A SPECIAL BOND

All at once the mare pulled free. Her eyes rolling wildly, she reared, then shied away.

"Grab her!" Frank called.

Stevie lunged for the lead shank but missed.

"No! Let me," Carole ordered. Instinct took over. She walked slowly toward the mare. She breathed in and out, in and out, willing the mare to sense the calming rhythm. She whispered nonsense words. Everyone watched as the mare stopped and listened to Carole. Carole inched closer. She reached out and stroked the mare's shoulder. Then she unclipped the lead line. She put it into her pocket. She knew she wouldn't need it. The mare followed Carole into the barn.

THE SADDLE CLUB

HORSE WHISPERS

BONNIE BRYANT

A SKYLARK BOOK
NEW YORK · TORONTO · LONDON · SYDNEY · AUCKLAND

RL 5, 009–012

HORSE WHISPERS

A Bantam Skylark Book / February 1998

ISBN 0-553-48624-1

Published simultaneously in the United States and Canada.

Bantam Books are published by Bantam Books, a division of Bantam Doubleday Dell
Publishing Group, Inc. Its trademark, consisting of the words "Bantam Books" and
the portrayal of a rooster, is Registered in U.S. Patent and Trademark Office and in
other countries. Marca Registrada. Bantam Books, 1540 Broadway, New York, New
York 10036.

PRINTED IN THE UNITED STATES OF AMERICA
OPM   0 9 8 7 6 5 4 3 2 1

*I would like to express my special thanks
to Caitlin Macy for her help
in the writing of this book.*

"WAKE UP, SLEEPYHEADS! Time to get up!" a voice called.

Stevie Lake stirred in her sleeping bag and cocked one eye open. "What time is it?" she croaked.

"Five of seven," murmured Lisa Atwood, half-asleep in the upper bunk.

"Ouch!" Carole Hanson said across the bunkhouse room. "That's uncivilized!"

The girls were used to getting up early for school, but this was vacation! They had arrived at the Bar None Ranch in Colorado very late the night before. Instead of going straight to bed, they had gone straight to the barn to visit their favorite horses.

"That's the one and only drawback to spending Febru-

1

ary break at a working ranch," Stevie groaned. "I can't get the sleep my growing body needs."

"You miss the eight hours, huh?" said Lisa, beginning to wake up in spite of herself.

"Eight?" Stevie scoffed. "Are you kidding? More like fifteen! We're talking the nine-to-noon schedule! I mean, if I wake up before—"

She was interrupted by a loud knock on the door. "Time to get up!" The voice paused. *"Breakfast is ready!"*

"Breakfast!" Stevie exclaimed, letting her previous thought go unfinished. "That's more like it!" In thirty seconds she was out of bed and yanking jeans and a sweater on over her long underwear. She flung the bunkhouse door open. "Wait up, Kate! I'm right behind you!" she yelled. She took off across the snow after the girls' friend and hostess at the ranch, Kate Devine.

Lisa and Carole sat up in bed and laughed. "I guess Stevie remembered the big plus about staying at the Bar None—the one that counterbalances the early hours," Lisa said.

"The food!" Carole guessed.

"Yup. Shall we?" said Lisa. "My stomach's growling."

"Mine too," Carole answered. Gritting her teeth, she sprang from bed into the frigid air of the bunkhouse, and Lisa followed suit.

It made Carole happy to hear Lisa sounding enthusiastic about eating. Unlike Stevie, who basically lived to eat,

Lisa had more complicated feelings about food. Not so long ago, she'd had a bout with near anorexia that had scared all three of the girls. Luckily Carole and Stevie had been able to help Lisa weather the problem. *The Saddle Club comes through again*, Carole thought, tying her long dark hair back in a ponytail.

The unique thing about the girls' friendship was that they weren't *just* friends, they were also members of a club called The Saddle Club, which they had started but which now included honorary out-of-town members such as Kate Devine. The club took its name from the girls' love of horses. But there was another important rule for joining: Members had to be willing to help each other out in any situation, whether that situation was a parental conflict, a boy problem, or something more serious.

"Come on, spacey! Quit zoning out, zip up that jacket, and we're outta here!" Lisa said.

Carole grinned. The other thing about The Saddle Club was that they all knew each other so well it was scary. Lisa was known for being a perfectionist, Stevie for her practical jokes, and Carole for spacing out about everything except horses. "Guilty as charged," she murmured, tailing Lisa out the door.

A few minutes later the two had joined Stevie, Kate, and the rest of the Bar None crew at breakfast. Meals were served in the main house's dining room on long tables. Because of the time of year, there were only a few hardy guests at the ranch, so everyone could fit at one table. Kate introduced The Saddle Club to two older couples, who nodded politely.

"Boy oh boy, that coffee smells good," said Stevie, sniffing the air appreciatively. "I can hardly wait."

Kate looked at her skeptically. "Since when do you drink coffee?"

"Oh, I don't *drink* it!" said Stevie. "I just—well, I *smell* it and it . . . it whets my appetite."

"As if the Lake appetite needed whetting!" Lisa protested.

At that moment Mrs. Devine emerged from the kitchen with a huge bowl of steaming hot cereal. "You might want to go easy on the oatmeal," she warned, "because this is only the beginning."

Undeterred, Stevie ladled herself a large portion, covered it with granola and raisins, and smothered the whole thing with cream.

Kate stood up and whispered something in her mother's ear.

"Yes, you may have the leftover apple pies for breakfast, too. I'm warming them now," replied Mrs. Devine.

"Pie? For breakfast? Why didn't you say so?" Stevie wailed. "I would have left out the raisins!"

For the next hour, Mrs. Devine shuttled back and forth between kitchen and dining room, refusing the girls' offers of help. After the oatmeal came scrambled eggs, Canadian bacon, corn muffins with homemade preserves, and the promised apple pies.

When they were stuffed and groaning, The Saddle Club agreed that, as usual, Kate's mother had outdone herself.

Even Lisa had managed to eat a full meal. Forking a last bite, she sighed and said, "If only I could cook like this."

"You *are* the best cook in the world, Mom," Kate said.

Stevie opened her mouth to add her vote but stopped. "I was about to agree, but I just realized I can't. No offense, but as a good daughter I have to say that *my* mother is the best cook in the world . . . Phyllis."

In Willow Creek the girls called each other's parents "Mrs. Lake" and "Mr. Atwood." But Phyllis and Frank had a firm rule at the Bar None: first names only. It made for a more casual atmosphere. Sometimes, though, it seemed strange, like right then when Stevie had hesitated before saying "Phyllis."

Kate and Stevie sparred teasingly for a couple of minutes, and Lisa chimed in to the debate. Then Lisa noticed that Carole wasn't saying anything. She felt a pang of remorse. Carole's mother had died a few years earlier. Maybe she felt left out. "Say, Carole?" she murmured.

To her relief, Carole looked up, utterly lost in thought. Then she smiled. "Oh, gosh, was I spacing again? I was thinking about Starlight's dressage test a few weeks ago. He really cut his corners."

Phyllis Devine and the girls laughed.

"What did I miss?" Carole asked sheepishly.

"We were debating over who the best cook in the world is," Lisa said.

"That's easy," said Carole. "My dad—but only when I help him."

"I'll bet you're a big help to him, the way Kate is to me," said Phyllis.

"I try to be. At first I didn't know anything, but now I can get around in the kitchen. After my mom died, we sort of learned together," Carole explained.

"Boy, I wish I could get around in the kitchen," Lisa muttered.

"You could learn," Phyllis responded. "Anyone can learn to cook, Lisa."

"Thanks," Lisa said without much enthusiasm. "But the problem is that I have to learn in about five days."

"Why? Are you having a dinner party?" Stevie teased. To her surprise, Lisa nodded.

"You are?"

"Yup. Well, not exactly a dinner party, but I have to cook a family meal over break."

"Why? Has your mom decided you should become a French chef?" Carole guessed. Mrs. Atwood was known for making Lisa learn "domestic skills" such as needlepoint and flower arranging.

"Hardly. In fact, cooking is the one thing she doesn't make me do—or even *let* me do. My mom's so perfect in the kitchen that she doesn't let me near the stove. No, this is for school. I have to cook the meal, take pictures of it, and write a report including all my recipes," Lisa explained with a sigh.

"Gosh, by the sound of your voice, I'd guess you had to catalog your stamp collection. But cooking's fun!" Phyllis said encouragingly.

"Maybe when it's *for* fun. But half of my home ec final grade is going to be based on this one meal," Lisa said, "and I can't even boil an egg!"

"Fiddlesticks," replied Phyllis.

"No, it's true! I tried and almost torched my teacher's hair!" Lisa wailed.

"Now, that sounds like a good idea," Stevie put in.

"Don't laugh! I'm getting a B-minus!" Lisa said. But then she started laughing, too. Another major difference between Lisa and Stevie was that while Stevie scraped by in school and prayed every day for a natural disaster to close the place for good, Lisa loved her classes and got straight As—at least, she usually did.

"Excuse me," said one of the female guests from the end of the table. "I couldn't help overhearing the conversation. I didn't know they even *offered* home economics at school anymore."

Lisa nodded unhappily. "In Willow Creek, Virginia, they *require* it," she said. "We have to take a semester each of home ec and shop. Only now home ec is called Nutrition and Household Management, and shop is called Advanced Woodworking. Boy, do I wish I were back sawing boards!"

"It's not fair," Stevie declared. "Public schools have all the fun! I would kill to take shop and home ec! But no, Fenton thinks every last class has to be an 'enriching academic experience.'"

At home in Willow Creek, Carole and Lisa attended the local public school, and Stevie went to a private day school, Fenton Hall.

"So you're saying you'd *like* to learn how to cook, Stevie?" Phyllis inquired.

"And how!" said Stevie. "I can make spaghetti and cookies and pancakes and stuff, but real food is over my head. Gosh, if I could make pies like these, I could feed myself all day long." She sighed blissfully at the thought.

"All right, that's a good enough reason. And Lisa, you *have* to learn," said Phyllis. "So why don't I teach both of you this week? There's no better place to learn than the Bar None kitchen. Heck, I've even taught cowboys how to cook!"

"Say, Mom," Kate piped up. "Couldn't Lisa make her big meal for the Bar None family? It doesn't have to be *your* family, does it, Lisa?"

Lisa shook her head. "No, I don't think so. The only rule is that I have to cook for at least four people." She laughed. "And I don't think that would be a problem here." The Bar None was known for its massive gatherings at mealtimes. The Devines often invited neighbors and employees to join in the festivities with their guests.

"Do you mean it?" Stevie asked. "You'd really teach us how to cook?"

"Of course I mean it! We'll start this afternoon."

"That would be great. I don't want to ask my mom because I know we'll get into a huge fight," Lisa said. This had already happened once. There was no way Lisa was going to deal with it again.

"And I don't want to ask *my* mom because my stupid brothers will make fun of everything I make and then they'll eat it all!" said Stevie.

At the other end of the table, the guests laughed. "Typical boys!" said a gray-haired woman, standing up to leave. "My brothers were exactly the same."

"Are you off for the day, Brenda?" Phyllis asked.

"Yes, we're going to head out," said the woman. All four of the guests thanked their hostess for the breakfast and excused themselves.

"Let me know if you need anything," Phyllis urged.

"I can't think of a thing," one of the husbands replied. "We're off to snowshoe right now, and we're going to eat lunch in town, so we probably won't see you till dinner." With a nod to the girls, the foursome left the dining room.

When they had gone, Phyllis poured herself another cup of coffee and sat back in her chair. "Gosh, I love old guests. The McHughs and the Martins have been coming here since we bought the place. I feel like they're almost family. They've been with us through thick and thin. And now they'll get to share a real *family* dinner with us." Then she added, looking at Lisa, "As long as you're game."

Lisa gulped. "I—I'm game. If you think I can do it."

"I know you can. Especially with Stevie as your helper. How about you, Carole, do you want to lend a helping hand?" Phyllis asked.

Stevie and Lisa glanced at their friend. From the doubtful expression on Carole's face, they knew she was thinking one thing and one thing only: Time spent in the kitchen was time away from the barn.

"You know what? I'd rather surprise Carole with our concoctions," Stevie said hurriedly. "She can be the taste tester."

Carole shot Stevie a thankful glance.

"That's an even better idea. Besides," Phyllis continued, her eyes twinkling to show she understood, "I wouldn't want to rob my husband of *all* his help in the barn."

"Speaking of Frank, where is he hiding this morning?" Carole asked. She was surprised that the head of the Bar None hadn't turned up for breakfast with them. Frank was as big a fan of his wife's cooking as The Saddle Club was, and with all the outdoor work he did, his appetite rivaled Stevie's.

"Dad's out at the barn," Kate replied. "He got a new load of horses in this morning at dawn. He and John and the other guys have been settling them in since then."

Carole's eyes lit up at the words *a new load of horses*. Lisa's eyes lit up at the name *John*. Both had to fight off an instinct to charge outside the way Stevie had at the mention of breakfast. The two of them started to talk at once.

"Where did the horses—"

"Did John say—"

They stopped, looked at each other, and burst out laughing.

Kate smiled knowingly. "Carole, the horses are from a dealer in Wyoming. He's done business with Dad before. There are five new ones, mares and geldings, all broken to saddle. Lisa, John has asked me ten times when you guys were arriving. He can't wait to see you."

The Saddle Club laughed some more. Even without hearing their questions, Kate had known how to answer.

Carole was so excited by the news of the horses that she automatically stood up and began to clear the breakfast dishes. Meanwhile she talked a mile a minute. "Five? Wow. Do you know anything about their breeding? How old are they? What colors? Do they go English and Western or just Western?" Laughing, Kate and Stevie helped her clear.

Phyllis tried to protest. "Girls, there'll be plenty of time to help out! Why don't you relax? This is your first day. I can get these."

But the girls insisted. Laden with plates, they trooped off to the kitchen.

Lisa sat for one last minute at the table. She stared out

the window at the snowbanks and gave a little sigh. John Brightstar was the son of the Devines' head wrangler. His heritage was Native American and his looks, Lisa thought with a pang, were tall, dark, and handsome. During the course of The Saddle Club's many visits to the ranch, Lisa had gotten to know him very well. They were friends, but they were something more than friends, too. Lisa was excited that John couldn't wait to see her. She couldn't wait to see him, either.

AFTER HELPING PHYLLIS load the oversize ranch dishwasher, The Saddle Club hurried back to the bunkhouse to change. It was very important to wear appropriate clothing in the barn. Looks didn't matter, but safety did, and most important was a pair of hard-soled shoes. Stevie always wore her ancient cowboy boots. Carole wore lace-up paddock boots. And Lisa switched between the English jodhpur boots her mother had bought her and the rubber-soled, leather-topped duck boots she preferred.

Kate came along to talk with the girls while they threw off their sneakers and dug around in their suitcases for barn shoes and extra sweaters.

"Do you remember if there was a gray in the new herd?" Lisa inquired.

Kate scrunched her face up. "You know, I think there might have been. I was half-asleep, so I didn't get the best look, but there's definitely one light-colored horse. I can't remember if it's a gray or a roan."

"I hope it's a gray! That's my favorite color," Lisa said. The other three girls groaned.

"But grays are so hard to keep clean!" Stevie said.

"Yeah, their hocks are permanently manure-stained," Kate added. As the girls knew, the term *gray* included horses that ranged in color from true gray to white. But even a horse that looked white was referred to as gray.

"I don't care," Lisa insisted. "It's still my favorite color."

"Why, Lisa? Is it because of Pepper?" Carole asked.

Lisa nodded, surprised that Carole had guessed so quickly. "That's right. Pepper is one of the best horses I've ever ridden. He taught me so much when I was a beginner. Now that he's gone, I guess I'm always looking for his replacement. Or not even his replacement—that would be impossible—but just another horse that would remind me of him. Since he was gray, I like grays the best."

Pepper, a dappled gray, had been a tried-and-true school horse at Pine Hollow, the girls' stable back home. As a beginner, Lisa had ridden Pepper often. The two had formed a special partnership. When Pepper was retired, Lisa had written a prizewinning essay about why he was such a great horse. A few months later, Pepper had had to be put down. But his memory lived on in the hearts of all the riders he had helped to train.

"A gray's fine for out West," Stevie said, trying to tame her dark blond hair into a ponytail, "where you don't have to scrub your horse spotless every other week for Pony Club competitions and shows. But back East, give me a nice dark bay or a liver chestnut any day. It's like my mom's theory on carpet: Never buy white or light pink, 'cause every stain shows. Get blue so you can relax."

"Sorry, Stevie, but I don't think there were any blue horses on the van this morning," Kate joked.

"There is such a thing as a blue roan, you know," Lisa pointed out, laughing.

"Right, but they only look blue because of black hairs running through the white. The other roans, bay roans and strawberry roans, like Berry, are more common," Carole said. Berry was the horse Carole usually rode out West. Her own horse, Starlight, was a bay, as was Stevie's horse, Belle.

The girls laughed.

"What?" Carole asked. Then she grinned sheepishly. "Oh. I'm sounding like a textbook again, aren't I?"

"Yes, but that's okay," Stevie said. "As long as you sound like a horsemanship textbook, I won't complain. But just *mention* algebra equations and I'm outta here!"

Carole giggled. "I'll try to keep my lectures limited to the subject of the equine."

Kate had been musing quietly as they talked. Now she spoke up tentatively. "It's funny how that works, isn't it?"

"How what works?" asked Lisa.

"Well, how for a lot of riders, there's one horse that was really special to them. And even if you ride a ton of other horses—better horses, more talented horses—that one horse stays with you. He always has a special place in your heart."

"Is yours one of your show horses?" Lisa asked. Once Kate had been a major junior rider on the top-level show circuit. She had owned and ridden several winners.

Kate shook her head. "Nope. I mean, I *loved* the hunters and equitation horses I had, every one of them. I still do, in fact. But I was thinking of the first pony I owned. She was a funny-looking buckskin named Black-Eyed Susan. I had her for eight months before I outgrew her. We sold her to a neighbor, and even after I got Butterscotch, my next horse, who was worth a lot more, I used to be jealous of the little girl next door because she got to ride Suzy. I don't know, something about our personalities clicked. And it's true, whenever I see a buckskin, I get kind of wistful." Kate stopped and cleared her throat. "Luckily, you don't see too many buckskins."

"What is buckskin? I'm not sure I know," said Lisa.

"It's a funny color," Kate answered. "Light chestnut with a black mane and tail. A lot of buckskins have a black stripe along their spine, too. Suzy did, anyway."

"That sounds cool!" Lisa responded. One of the best

16

things about hanging out with The Saddle Club—and its extended family—was that she never stopped learning. Kate, Stevie, and Carole had all been riding practically since they were born. Lisa had come to the sport later. She had caught up fast and could hold her own in the saddle, but there were still things she didn't know. That was why horses were so amazing. Even Carole agreed that you could never learn it all.

Dressed and ready, the girls headed out to the stable. On their way they saw a tall figure approaching them at a jog. Lisa recognized him at once.

"Hi, everyone!" John Brightstar called. His face was ruddy from exertion.

"Hey!" they all said.

"Hi, John," Lisa added quietly.

John and Lisa didn't give each other big hugs or anything like that. Both of them were very private people who didn't like to make a display of their friendship. But John gave Lisa a special look that made her spine tingle.

"I came to show you guys where the new horses are corralled. I figured you'd want to say hi to them," said John. He turned and fell into step beside Lisa.

"We were just talking about colors of horses, John," Kate said. "We all seem to have a favorite."

John nodded. "Most horsepeople do. Of course, we all know bright chestnut is the best," he said, pretending to be serious. His own horse, Tex, was a chestnut.

"Naturally," Lisa said, elbowing him in the ribs.

17

"Hey!" said John. He elbowed her playfully in response. "You know, in the old days they used to think that a horse's color had an effect on his personality."

Stevie raised her eyebrows. "But it does!" she exclaimed, indignant.

"You really believe that, Stevie?" Lisa asked. "You really believe the way a horse acts is related to his color?"

"Of course!" said Stevie. "You can't tell me that Stewball would be Stewball if he hadn't been born with a splashy pinto coat."

That was a tough point to deny. Stewball was one of the ranch horses. He was kooky and sometimes seemed half crazy. But he was also an expert cattle horse, the best on the Bar None at roping and herding. The main reason he was so good at his job was that he was totally stubborn, with a mind of his own. Not surprisingly, he and Stevie had hit it off from day one. Now she always rode him when The Saddle Club visited.

"It *is* hard to imagine Stewball any other color," Lisa admitted. "I mean, I just can't see him as a bay or a chestnut."

"See?" Stevie said. "Color's got everything to do with it."

John looked doubtful. "What do you think of all this nonsense, Carole?" he asked.

"Yeah, Carole," Kate urged. A lot of times the group deferred to Carole on matters of horsemanship. She was not only an excellent rider, she had also read everything available on the subject of horses. And she had a real horsewoman's common sense and intuition.

At the sound of her name, Carole snapped to attention. "I'm sorry, Kate, what did you say?" she asked.

The girls and John turned as a group to look at her. Her voice sounded odd—choked up.

"Um, I was just wondering what you thought about, you know, whether a horse's color means anything," Kate said gently.

"Oh. Yes," Carole said slowly. "I think maybe it does. I know that's not very scientific, but . . ." Her voice trailed off as she stared at the ground. Abruptly she looked up again. "I hope one of the horses is black—Cobalt black."

"I like black, too," John responded. "It's such a majestic color. I think every kid dreams of having a Black Beauty of his own. . . ." He chattered away, unaware that Lisa's and Stevie's minds were racing.

Before either of them could say anything, the group had neared the holding pen where the new horses were corralled.

"Look at that chestnut!" Kate cried. "He's cute, huh?"

"Oh, there's the gray!" Lisa pointed. "I call dibs! And look at the markings on that bay. *Four* white stockings!"

"Gosh, that Appaloosa is fat! What do you think they've been feeding him?" Stevie asked.

Reaching the fence, the five of them pulled themselves up onto the lower rail. With the extra height they could lean over the fence and get a better look at the newcomers.

"The Appy's a mare," said Kate. "And I think my dad said she's been sitting around for a couple of years not doing a thing."

"We'll have to get her back into training, then," Stevie said. "Diet and exercise, huh, baby?" She leaned farther over the fence and extended a hand, trying to coax the mare closer. "Here, girl, come say hi."

In response the mare swished her tail lazily. Except for that and flicking an ear, she didn't move. Stevie laughed. "So much for my powers of persuasion! One word from me and she stays right where she is. I wish I had some treats— a carrot or something. Carole, you try," she urged. Often Carole could get a horse to come to her when the others failed.

"Sure, Stevie." Carole clucked through her teeth. "Here, pretty girl, come on. We want to say hi, girl. That's right, mosey on over. We want to be your—" Midsentence, Carole stopped. She stared straight ahead, all thoughts of the Appaloosa forgotten. Her throat felt dry. She closed her eyes and reopened them. She couldn't believe what she was seeing. It was as if her dreams had materialized before her. At the other side of the corral, not twenty feet away, was a tall black mare. She was standing slightly apart from the rest of the herd. Her nose was raised to the wind. She was coal black, as black as night. . . . Carole felt her heart racing: She was *Cobalt* black. She looked exactly like the stallion, only smaller. She had his large eyes, his sloping shoulder and compact body. They could have been brother and sister, the resemblance was so strong. She had everything but his markings. Carole felt so shaky she had to step down to the ground. She leaned weakly against the fence.

Lisa and Stevie had seen it all. Ignoring Kate's and John's inquiring looks, they stepped off the fence. "Are you okay, Carole?" Lisa murmured.

"I'm—I'm fine," Carole said. Her voice came out in a whisper. "It's just that mare. She looks exactly like . . ."

Carole didn't finish the sentence, but it didn't matter: Lisa and Stevie understood. Later they would have to fill in Kate and John about Cobalt, but for now they wanted to comfort their friend. There was no question Cobalt was the horse that Carole had never gotten over—and probably never would.

A beautiful black stallion, Cobalt had performed best when Carole rode him, even though he belonged to someone else. His owner was the ultra-spoiled Veronica di-Angelo. Veronica badly mishandled the horse. One day she made one mistake too many. She set Cobalt at a fence all wrong. It was impossible for him to jump clean. The beloved stallion had fallen and broken his leg. There was no choice but to put him down. What made it worse was that Cobalt's death had followed the death of Carole's mother. It had shaken Carole to the core, so much so that she had quit riding for a while. All that was a long time ago. Now Carole owned—and loved—Starlight. But in the back of her mind, an image of the black stallion still lingered. And the mare in front of her was a living, breathing version of that image.

Drawing a shaky breath, Carole climbed up on the fence again. "She looks a lot like a horse I once knew," she said, trying to make her voice sound normal. "It—It freaked me out for a minute."

The black mare swiveled her ears back and forth. She paced along the fence and then stopped. She appeared to be listening for some specific sound. "It's okay," Carole murmured, willing the horse to understand. The mare turned uncertainly toward the group on the fence. "You'll be fine," Carole said.

The mare took a nervous step forward.

"All right, you guys, feeding time!" called a stable boy. The mare shied violently. She trotted to the other end of the corral, snorting loudly. Carole bit her lip in frustration.

The boy slipped through the fence rails. He had a bucket of grain and was shaking it loudly. All the horses except for the black mare turned their heads and started to amble toward him. The mare stayed where she was, tense and ready to bolt.

"We're going to put them in the standing stalls for the afternoon," Kate explained. "They'll live in the big pasture and come and go as they want. But since they're going to be guest mounts, they have to get used to spending part of the day inside. Wanna help bring them in?"

"You bet," said Lisa. Together they walked around to the gate. The stable boy had started to clip lead shanks to the horses' halters.

"We always leave the halters on for the first few days," Kate continued. "That way if a new horse panics, gets loose, or gets into a bad situation, there's something to grab."

Taking a look down the corral, Carole offered, "Maybe I should try to get the mare in, the black mare, I mean. She looks like she might be a little shy."

"Yeah, you're right," Kate replied. "She doesn't look too happy about coming inside, does she?" They all turned to look at the mare. She was sniffing the air and pacing. "Why don't you give it a shot? The less hassle these horses give us, the happier Dad will be about his investment."

"Did somebody say Dad?" boomed a deep, friendly voice. The girls spun around. Frank Devine was emerging from the nearby stable. He came up and gave each of them a bear hug. "You keeping these girls in line?" he asked John.

"Yes, sir," said John, his dark eyes twinkling.

"Good, because I wouldn't want these dudes to get into trouble," Frank warned.

The girls laughed. On their first trip out to the ranch, they had learned the word *dudes*. It was a word that cowboys and ranchers used to refer to novices, Easterners usually, who didn't know the first thing about Western riding and ranch work. The girls *had* been dudes at one time, but now they were seasoned enough to know that Frank was only kidding.

"Maybe this afternoon I'll teach 'em how to saddle up and mount," John joked.

"Would you, John?" Stevie asked breathlessly. "That would be just swell!"

Everyone laughed again except for Frank. His attention had wandered to the corral. "Why is that mare still standing there? I want all the horses in—and pronto. I missed my wife's breakfast and I *don't* intend to miss her lunch!"

"She doesn't seem to want to come in, Dad," Kate explained. "Carole just volunteered to go and get her."

"Thanks, Carole, but if she's going to be trouble, why don't you leave her to one of the wranglers? You girls can take these four in"—Frank gestured to the horses assembled at the gate—"and Mick, here, will follow with the black. Okay?"

Carole nodded. Frank was not only Kate's father and the boss of the ranch, he was also their host at the Bar None. To argue with him would be rude. But instead of going and taking another horse's lead, she let Stevie, Kate, Lisa, and John get ahead. They each took a horse from the stable boy, Mick, and moved off in a group, talking animatedly about the new arrivals. Carole hung back to watch. The minutes ticked away as first Mick, then Frank had a go at catching the mare. Mick tried coaxing her with grain. Frank tried speaking to her while he crept closer. Nothing they did seemed to make a difference. The mare would wait until they were a few yards away; then she would spin and dash to another part of the paddock, forcing them to start all over.

"If I were mounted with a rope on me, I'd lasso her and that would be that," said Mick in frustration.

"Ah, well, don't sweat it. It's not your fault. She's probably shaken up after the van ride," Frank said. "We'll leave her be for another few hours and try again this afternoon."

"Could I try?" Carole said. She was worried that Frank would be mad at her for lagging behind. To her relief, the older man smiled.

"I like your persistence, Carole. Sure, why not? Mick, give her the lead shank."

Looking surprised, the stable boy handed over the white cotton line. Carole took it and paused, chewing on her lip. She knew she wouldn't be able to catch the mare if the men stayed. Somehow she sensed they would scare the horse off. But she couldn't exactly ask them to leave. That would sound cocky beyond belief!

Wondering what to do, Carole missed what Frank said next. "Sorry?" she said. "I didn't hear you."

"I said, good luck, but don't waste a lot of time if you can't get her. Go in and have fun with Kate and the girls. Come on, Mick, we've gotta go see about that water pipe."

"Right, boss."

"See you at lunch, Carole. Noon, straight up. Don't be late," Frank added.

"I won't be," Carole said absently. She took a deep breath and walked toward the mare.

3

EVER SO SLOWLY, Carole let her breath out. She concentrated on the mare, trying to communicate a sense of calm. The mare tossed her head up and down. She snorted. But she stood her ground. Approaching at a snail's pace, Carole was beside the horse a few minutes later. She looked the mare deep in the eyes. She breathed in and out. "Easy does it," she murmured. "I'm not going to hurt you. I knew a horse like you once—so much like you that you could have been twins. What do you think of that, hmmm?" Carole stretched out her hand and stroked the black coat. All the while, she spoke in a low, soothing voice so that the mare would trust her.

"You need some serious grooming, don't you, girl?

Pretty soon we're going to get you inside and curry you and brush you till you shine like a black pearl. That's right—nobody's going to hurt you at the Bar None. Everyone's your friend here. I am and Kate is and Kate's father . . ."

As Carole went on talking and rubbing the mare's neck, a thought suddenly occurred to her. She had been assuming that the previous owners were to blame for the horse's being people-shy. She'd been guessing that they had been rough with her, or worse. But something about that theory didn't fit. The mare didn't seem abused so much as plain afraid of being caught. She wasn't exhibiting any of the signs of an animal that has *learned* to mistrust people: She wasn't laying her ears back or baring her teeth. She seemed to mistrust people instinctively. Carole made a mental note of the fact. She didn't see how it would help, but it was always good to know as much as possible about a horse that you wanted to train. Sometimes knowing one little thing—like the fact that a horse was petrified of water, say—could save years of exasperation.

Carole lingered a long time with the mare. She patted her and scratched her withers. She took her gloves off. Even though her hands were soon freezing, she pulled burrs from the black mane and straightened it with her fingers. The cold began to seep into her skin, through the many layers of clothing, but Carole persisted. Finally, after a long time, Carole clipped the lead shank to the mare's halter. She didn't try to bring her in right away, though.

Instead she led her gently back and forth across the corral, asking her to walk and halt, walk and halt. Finally the mare seemed to relax. When the refined black head was lowered in boredom, Carole knew that she had gained the mare's trust. Only then did she lead the horse inside to a waiting stall.

On the way in, the mare stopped and put her head down to the ground. She foraged with her hoof, pawing at the snow till she found a tiny shoot underneath. Carole studied her movements. She was surprised that a domesticated horse would go to such lengths to get a bite of grass.

Before leaving, she made sure there were water and hay in the stall.

"I promise I'll come back this afternoon, but right now I've got to go in myself and eat lunch." Carole glanced at her watch to make sure she was on time. She caught her breath with a start: It was half past twelve—half an hour late—and she wasn't even ready!

LUNCH WAS NEARLY over. Frank took a last sip of coffee, wiped his mouth, and pushed his chair back from the table. Lisa and Stevie held their breath, praying he hadn't noticed Carole's absence. Kate's father wasn't a strict man, but he didn't like guests—even guests like The Saddle Club—running around the ranch getting lost and missing meals. It was a formula for trouble.

"I have to hand it to Carole," Frank said. The girls exchanged worried glances. "She's even more horse-crazy

29

than I would have believed." He chuckled. "I left her out there an hour ago with that black mare, and I'll be darned if she isn't still trying to catch her."

"Oh, I'll bet she's caught her by now," Lisa said confidently.

Frank looked at her, surprised. "You think so?"

Lisa nodded vigorously. "Absolutely. Carole can catch anything that moves. She probably started talking to the mare and lost track of time."

Stevie seconded her friend. "Yup. Happens all the time at Pine Hollow. We'll be waiting for her, thinking she's in trouble, and instead she's just sitting in Starlight's stall having a conversation."

Frank laughed heartily. "A conversation? But that would mean the horses talk back."

"They sort of do," said Lisa. "Not the way you'd think, but I swear Carole understands them." She could tell by Frank's expression that he didn't quite believe her. "It's true," she insisted. "It's just . . . It's just this weird thing," she finished lamely. *Heck*, she thought, *I wouldn't have believed it myself if I hadn't seen Carole get through to difficult horses so many times before.* Still, Lisa was pleased to see that John Brightstar had a thoughtful expression on his face: *He* believed her, at least.

"I'll put a plate of food in the oven for Carole," Phyllis volunteered. "I'm sure she'll want it when she remembers. Now, are you girls ready for pie-making lesson number one?"

Stevie stood up from the table. "As ready as we'll ever be, ma'am," she declared, imitating a soldier going off to combat.

Kate, Frank, and John helped clear before heading their separate ways. Frank went to his office to do some paperwork. John went out to the ranch truck: He had to run some errands in town. At her parents' insistence, Kate went to her room to do a couple of hours of homework. "But Mom—"

"Don't 'but Mom' me," said Phyllis. "That was part of our agreement: Even with your friends visiting, you've got to get some work done."

"Yes, Mom," Kate said, sighing.

Lunch cleanup took no time at all. Phyllis explained that she tried to tidy up after herself as she cooked. That way, the only things to be done after the meal were stacking the dishwasher and putting food away. "Of course, it doesn't always work, especially when I'm busy, but it's a good principle, anyway." She paused to flip through her recipe box. "Now, I thought we'd start with a classic: a nice, simple, one-crust pumpkin pie that you can impress your mothers with next Thanksgiving. The filling's a snap, so we can concentrate on the crust." After a moment's search, she took out a tattered card and clipped it to the refrigerator. Just then the telephone rang.

"Hello, Bar None." Stevie and Lisa watched as Phyllis's face changed from anticipation to resignation. "I see. . . . Of course. . . . No, please! It's no trouble at all." Jotting a note down on a piece of paper, she hung up the phone. "Girls, I'm so sorry, but I'm afraid that we're going to have to postpone the lesson. I've got to go on a little rescue mission."

"It's nothing serious, is it?" Lisa asked, envisioning a guest with a broken leg, then a cow stuck in a ravine.

"No, thank God. It's just that Brenda has discovered that after six months of sitting at a desk, she's not in great shape. They're in town and she doesn't feel up to snow-shoeing back."

"So you're going to go get her?" Stevie asked, horrified. "Boy, I'd make her walk!"

Mrs. Devine smiled. "Unfortunately, I don't think that would make the Bar None very popular with the McHugh family. Anyway, it's just a half hour's drive into town." She sighed. "I only wish they had called five minutes ago. I could have asked John to give her a ride. But this is what running a guest ranch is like—you have to be flexible." Phyllis removed her apron and hung it on a nail beside the refrigerator. "We'll try again tomorrow, okay?"

"Great," Stevie said.

"Keep an eye on the oven, will you?" Phyllis added over her shoulder. "I've got Carole's leftovers warming."

"Sure thing," Lisa called. Even a little task like that made her feel professional.

When Phyllis was gone, the girls gave the kitchen counters a final wipe. Both of them felt bad that she had been called away. They wanted to leave the kitchen as spotless as possible. On her second go-round, the pie recipe caught Stevie's eye. She went to the fridge and read it over. It didn't look like there was much to it. "Say, Lis'—" she began.

Lisa glanced at her friend. She could already tell what Stevie had in mind. "No way!"

"But Lisa—"

"Forget it. I am not going to make the pie without Phyllis, so you can just drop the subject right now."

Stevie smiled. Some people had an inborn talent for talking to horses. She, Stevie Lake, had an inborn talent for talking to her friends—and persuading them to do things they didn't want to do. "Of course *you're* not going to make the pie," she said in her most wheedling voice. "We're *both* going to make the pie."

"No, Stevie—"

"You heard what Phyllis said: a nice, simple, one-crust pumpkin pie. How hard can it be?"

Lisa crossed her arms over her chest defensively. She was all too familiar with Stevie's powers of persuasion. "*Very* hard," she answered. "Very, very, very, very hard."

"Listen to this: The only ingredients in the crust are butter, flour, and water. Don't you think we can handle that?"

Lisa frowned. She had to admit she was surprised. "That's it? That's all that makes a crust?"

Stevie saw her window of opportunity and jumped. "Can you believe it? Three ingredients! It'll be a piece of cake—I mean, pie! Think how great it will taste—"

"Stevie—"

"I mean, think how impressed Phyllis will be—and everyone—when we serve it for dessert tonight! We'll be helping out in a big way. Phyllis is having such a busy day, and this will be one less thing she'll have to worry about." Stevie eyed Lisa shrewdly. She could tell her friend was wavering. It was time for the kill. "Think of how impressed a certain *ranch hand* will be."

Lisa's eyebrows flew up. "A certain ranch hand . . . Now who could that be? I don't know what you're— Oh, *John!*" She grinned. "I'm not even sure he has a sweet tooth," she said coyly.

Stevie looked unconvinced by Lisa's theatrics. She opened the refrigerator door and took out a stick of butter. She opened the pantry and took out a canister of flour.

Lisa watched her, chewing on a nail. She felt herself weakening. "Oh, okay!" she burst out. "I give in! Let's make the pie ourselves. You're right. How hard can it be?"

Stevie congratulated Lisa on her decision. And she silently congratulated herself on her ability to influence her friends. Obviously it was as sharp as ever. " 'Preheat the oven to three-fifty,' " she read.

"Got it," Lisa said. "What next?"

"It's strange. We're supposed to 'cut' the butter into the flour."

"Cut?" Lisa asked dubiously.

"Cut," Stevie affirmed.

The two girls looked at one another. They had the tiniest inkling that they were about to get more than they had bargained for. But this was no time for thinking negatively.

"It probably just means mash them together," Lisa guessed.

Stevie frowned. "All right. That's easy enough."

Stevie got two big steak knives out of a drawer and proceeded to chop the stick of butter into tiny pieces, humming as she worked. Then she poured the flour Lisa had measured over the butter. She mashed the mixture with a fork. "The most important thing about cooking is that you've really got to get into it," she announced. "No holding back." She laid the fork down and started using her hands.

Lisa watched her skeptically. "Isn't that kind of . . . germy?" she asked.

"Germy, schmermy!" Stevie replied, scraping dough from her wrists. "All right, we're ready for the water."

Lisa consulted the recipe. "Okay. Three tablespoons of ice water, coming right up."

"Three tablespoons? That's it? That must be a mistake. Who ever heard of a recipe calling for *spoons* of water? I'll bet they mean cups," Stevie said confidently. "Pour it in whenever you're ready."

Lisa poured about a cup of water into the flour-butter

mixture. Then she stopped. Why was she trusting Stevie's advice on the amounts? "That's all I'm adding," she announced. "It looks like too much already."

"Too much? What do you mean?" Stevie said indignantly.

Lisa pointed. "Look. The dough is all wet and . . . pasty," she said.

Stevie laughed dismissively. "That's because we haven't chilled it yet. Come on, into the fridge with you," she said, trying to gather the wet dough into a ball. "Aaah! It's alive!"

Lisa turned to see Stevie attempting to stop the dough from slipping through her fingers. With loud plops, two blobs of it landed on the floor.

"Gross!" Lisa screamed. A piece of it had jumped up and hit her cheek.

Ignoring her, Stevie shoved the rest of the dough onto a piece of waxed paper, the waxed paper onto a cookie sheet, and the cookie sheet into the fridge. "All right, now we wait an hour while—" Stevie's foot hit the spilled dough and slid forward a yard.

"Gee, I didn't know you could do a split!" Lisa joked.

Stevie glowered. She pushed herself back up. "As I was saying, we wait an hour—"

"Say, couldn't we move the dough to the freezer and then wait just a half hour?" Lisa suggested. Her practical mind was always trying to think of shortcuts.

Stevie thought. "Why not?" She took the ball of dough

from the refrigerator and opened the freezer door above. A large frozen steak came shooting out and hit the floor. Lisa grinned. Stevie glared. Lisa picked up the steak and handed it solemnly to Stevie. Stevie tried to put it back into the freezer, but another steak slid out. "Here, you pick up—"

The cookie sheet of dough slid out, sloshing water. "Aaarrgh!" Stevie yelled, stamping her foot. It took the two of them about ten minutes to rearrange everything so that the freezer door would shut.

"Let's play Go Fish while we wait for the dough to chill," Lisa suggested.

"Great idea."

A half hour later, the girls ran to the kitchen, playing cards in hand. "It looks like a frozen potato stuck in an ice chip," Lisa wailed when she saw the results. "How are we ever going to roll it out?"

"Don't worry," Stevie reassured her. "We'll chop it down to size." She grabbed a knife and began hacking at the frozen crust. "Take that, you stupid crust!"

Lisa chuckled. Bits of ice flew through the air. One hit Lisa on the shoulder. Stevie laughed. "Watch out for flying frozen pie crust," she murmured.

"Ha-ha," said Lisa sarcastically. On an impulse she picked up a handful of flour and blew it at Stevie's back.

Stevie grinned. She knew a challenge when she saw one. She took a chunk of crust and lobbed it at Lisa.

Lisa ducked; the crust hit the wall. "Is that in the

recipe, too?" she inquired. "Are you supposed to 'toss' the crust?"

Stevie snorted in spite of herself. "Yeah, first you toss it, and then you juggle it!" She picked up another three chunks and proceeded to juggle. One by one they hit the floor. "Hey, did you hear the way they landed? I've got rhythm!"

"Stevie, really," Lisa deadpanned, "I thought you knew better. You can't roll out the crust on the floor!"

"Oh yes I can!" Stevie said, dropping to the floor and doing a forward roll on top of the melting crust.

Lisa cracked up. "But the recipe says you're supposed to *flour* the surface first," she reminded Stevie. She took what was left in the bag of flour and dumped it on top of Stevie's head.

"Say, Lisa, wasn't this supposed to be a joint effort? I thought we were doing it *together*," Stevie said, yanking Lisa down to the floor.

Lisa tried to sit up. She was laughing too hard. The butter wrapper had fallen on the floor. Somehow Lisa felt that Stevie's face needed a good greasing, and now was the time. She stretched out her hand . . .

"Don't even try it, Atwood!" Stevie yelled. She sprang to her feet, brandishing a long fork at Lisa. *"En garde!"*

Lisa pawed the floor. She snorted and galloped toward Stevie on her hands and knees. In the middle of her charge, she stopped. Instead of Stevie's faded jeans and boots, she was face to face with a pair of gray wool slacks and black shoes. Lisa gulped. She looked from the shoes to the trouser legs to the knees. Then she sat back on her heels and looked up. Phyllis Devine was smiling down at her.

At that moment Stevie spun around, waving the apron. "Hey, Lis'! Here's your red flag!" she shouted. Then she stopped dead in her tracks. Kate's mother was standing in the doorway with Carole behind her. Carole was trying very hard to keep a straight face but was only partly succeeding. Stevie felt flour cascading down her back.

Lisa looked up at her imploringly.

"Oh, hello," Stevie said nonchalantly. "We were just, you know, making a nice, simple, one-crust pie."

4

PHYLLIS STARTED LAUGHING so hard, tears ran down her face. "I wish I had my camera!" she cried. "This is one for the ranch scrapbook!"

As she went on cracking up, Lisa sniffed. "All we were trying to do was make a pie!"

"Yeah—we were going to surprise you," Stevie mumbled. The two of them were embarrassed beyond belief.

"I have to say, I admire your spunk," Phyllis said when she had managed to stop guffawing. "But next time, wait for me, okay?"

Stevie and Lisa nodded shamefacedly.

"Hey!" Phyllis said. "Why the hangdog expressions?

Come on, let's get this place whipped into shape. Do you mind?" She pointed to her apron.

"Oh, ah, no, not at all," Stevie said, relinquishing the "red flag."

Phyllis swiftly tied it on. "We've got dinner to prepare. I'm serving vegetable soup and I need two choppers."

"I'll help you guys clean up," Carole volunteered. Crossing in front of her friends, she couldn't hold back a giggle.

"Watch it, Hanson," Stevie growled. "This pie-making isn't as easy as it sounds."

"Yeah," Lisa added. "Have you ever tried making a crust?"

"Once," Carole said. "Dad and I ended up looking just like you. Now we always buy ready-made crusts."

"Say, Carole," Phyllis said, "I'll bet you're hungry. I saved some lunch for you. It's right here in the oven." She reached for the oven door.

Too late Stevie realized what they had done. "Oh, no!" she cried. "We forgot—!" A huge cloud of black smoke poured out. Warily Phyllis held up a plate of charred food. Carole's leftovers were burned to a crisp.

Knowing they couldn't sink any lower, Lisa mumbled, "We turned the oven up to preheat it for the crust."

"Yeah," Stevie added. "Unfortunately, the crust never reached the oven stage. So we, uh, cooked your grilled cheese for about an hour and twenty minutes."

Phyllis put the plate down on the stove. She reached up to turn on the oven fan. "I think maybe tomorrow we'll learn how to boil water," she said dryly.

CAROLE MADE HERSELF another sandwich while Stevie and Lisa chopped vegetables. Then Phyllis banished them all to the barn. Kate had finished her reading and came down to join them. She laughed when she heard about the pie fiasco. "Now, if you had only started a fire, then you would have lived up to my kitchen diaster. As it is, I think yours is only about second or third best," she joked.

The plan for the afternoon was to saddle up the new horses and try them out. They would have to be ridden a few times by different people before Frank considered them safe for guests. It would be the girls' job to say whether a particular horse should be assigned to a beginner, to an intermediate, or only to an advanced rider. Even then the Devines were very careful. Many a time they had heard a guest brag about his riding abilities only to find him trying to get on from the right side of the horse!

Walking out to the stables, the girls noticed that the sky was beginning to cloud over. The Rocky Mountains, which were majestic in the sun, were barely visible now. "Is it going to snow later?" Lisa asked, hoping it wouldn't ruin their plans.

"Yes, we're supposed to get six to eight inches tonight," Kate replied. She paused and squinted up. "But I'm betting it will hold off for a couple of hours. I've gotten pretty good at predicting the weather out here, and that sky isn't ready to start dumping white stuff yet."

"Good, then let's hustle," said Lisa.

In the barn the girls had a quick discussion. They decided to groom and saddle up four of the horses and take them for a brief ride. They would leave the black mare for last in case she was still spooked.

"I'll just check on her and then I'll join you guys," Carole said.

Stevie and Lisa watched her walk off in the direction of the mare's stall. Neither of them said what they were both thinking: *Carole's already getting attached.*

"If no one else cares, I'll take the gray, okay?" said Lisa.

"Great," Kate replied. "I want the chestnut gelding. He and I are already becoming friends."

"Okay, so I'll take Mrs. Fat Appaloosa, which leaves Carole with the bay," said Stevie.

In no time at all the three girls were hard at work. They curried, brushed, and picked hooves. They wiped out the horses' nostrils and checked their ears. It was cold in the barn, so they were all glad of the physical exertion.

After a visit to the black mare, Carole joined them. She was distracted, but she tried not to let it show. The mare hadn't touched the hay or water in her stall—a typical sign of being ill at ease.

"Hey, we've been calling these horses 'the bay' and 'the

chestnut.' But what are their real names?" Lisa inquired, giving the gray a final rub with her rag.

"Yeah," said Stevie. "I'm beginning to feel impolite."

Kate grinned. "Sorry—bad habit. I'm so used to having to point out the horses to the guests by color that sometimes I forget they actually have names. The gray is Merry, Lisa; the bay is Cardinal, the Appy's called Chocolate Chips, and this guy is Be a Gentleman, Gent for short."

"How do you do, Gent?" Stevie said. She picked up his near foreleg at the ankle and pretended to shake it. "Gee, some manners," she said. "He didn't even answer!"

When the horses had been saddled, the girls brought them back out to the corral. There was snow on the ground, but it had been packed down enough to make riding possible. And none of these horses was shod, so the snow wouldn't ball up in their hooves.

The girls mounted and put the horses through their (Western) paces: walk, jog, and lope. They stopped and turned them, neck-reining and using vocal commands. They even made some "bad rider" mistakes on purpose to see how the horses would react. Then they switched horses. At this point, something became clear: Each of the girls had developed a loyalty to her first horse.

"This Appy is *slow*," Lisa complained. She was using all her energy to urge the poky, overweight horse into a jog.

"She's not slow, she's just quiet!" Stevie cried indignantly. "Use your legs more!" She sat back in her own saddle to ask the gray to walk. The horse promptly speeded up. "Boy, this gray is no beginner horse!" Stevie remarked scornfully.

"Excuse me? Merry is fine for beginners! Even a beginner can't just sit there and let the horse do whatever he wants!" Lisa retorted.

Across the corral, Kate was struggling to turn the splashy bay. The horse was resisting and walking straight ahead. "This guy needs some brushing up, doesn't he? He's like a kid who's been out of school too long!"

Passing, aboard the chestnut Gent, Carole scoffed loudly. "That's what I was going to say about this horse. He's—He's—" but Carole couldn't think of a complaint.

Lisa had to laugh. Even her own comments had sounded funny. She called everyone to the middle of the ring. "I think we've got to switch one more time to make a fair assessment of these horses," she said.

Everyone agreed. After fifteen minutes aboard their next mounts, the girls hopped down and led the horses back to the stable for untacking—and judgment. They decided that the Appaloosa, Chips, was lazy but safe, a perfect beginner horse. Merry, the gray that Lisa liked, was high-strung but not dangerous. He didn't shy, buck, rear, or do anything but try to go faster than the rider wanted: a good intermediate mount. The bay was stubborn but quiet: advanced beginner. The chestnut got three thumbs up. He was a wonderful horse—attractive, obedient, energetic, even comfortable: an ideal mount for many levels of rider.

"I think Dad's going to be really pleased with his purchases," Kate commented. "He's always trusted this dealer, and I can see why. These four are going to be a great addition to the Bar None fleet."

"Four? You mean five," Carole reminded her, amazed that Kate could forget the most eye-catching horse of the bunch. "There's the black mare."

"How could I forget?" Kate said. "And we haven't even tried her!"

"Let's all go groom her," Lisa suggested.

"Yeah, we can give her the deluxe treatment," Stevie joked. "Full facial, manicure, pedicure . . ."

Carole pursed her lips. Her friends were so enthusiastic that she didn't want to say anything. But she was afraid of how the mare would react to getting attention from four people at once.

"Carole?" said Kate, seeing Carole's brow wrinkle. "A penny for your thoughts?"

Carole thought quickly. "Oh! I was just, um, wondering . . . what the real name of the mare is," she said.

"Hey, that's right. You never told us *her* name," said Lisa.

Kate screwed up her face in concentration. "You know, I'm not sure I know. We'll have to ask Dad."

The girls trooped down the aisle to the mare's stall. In the East, most horses lived inside and spent the nights in large box stalls. But out West, the horses weren't babied as much. At the Bar None the majority lived outside in a big pasture. There was a shed in the pasture that the horses could wander into for protection from the elements. It was a lot less work for the wranglers (who had far fewer stalls to muck), and it was a more natural way for horses to live—closer to their original habitat. Carole was glad of that. She sensed that the black mare would be happy to get out of her stall as soon as possible. Now if only she wouldn't freak when she saw the group of them.

"What on earth—" Stevie stopped and stared. The mare's stall door was open. She peered inside. Sure enough, the stall was empty.

Lisa was right behind her. "She's gone!"

"THIS *IS* THE stall you put her in, isn't it?" Kate asked.

Carole nodded, her heart pounding. "Yes. Last stall on the left. I'm positive."

Automatically the girls turned and looked down the aisle. The main door at the end of the stable was wide open. "Oh no," Carole murmured, her fears mounting.

In summer the big sliding door was open all the time. In winter it was open a couple of times a day, when the stable boys went back and forth to the manure pile with wheelbarrows. Clearly, the mare had escaped from her stall and walked right out of the barn.

Carole sprinted to the open door. If she hurried . . . ! Snow was beginning to fall, a few flakes at a time. On the muddy ground, hoofprints led off in the direction of the pasture. Carole didn't wait to explain. That would take valuable minutes. She started off in hot pursuit.

At the stall Kate was leaning in, examining the door. "She must have worked the bolt with her mouth, huh, Carole? I should have thought! We've had horses do that before." She stood up. "Carole?"

"She took off toward the big pasture!" said Lisa, hurrying outside.

Just then Mick and John appeared around the corner of the barn. They were pushing empty wheelbarrows. "I thought you girls were going riding," said John. He paused, letting the snow land on his head and shoulders.

"We were—I mean, we did," Lisa replied hurriedly. "And we were about to try the black mare."

"And?" said Mick. "She looked like she was calming down a little when we passed by, didn't she, John?"

John nodded. "Definitely. It may take a while, but she'll adjust."

Lisa rushed to make herself clear. "No—but she took off. She escaped!"

"And Carole took off to look for her," Stevie added.

Mick and John exchanged worried looks. "Does the boss know?" Mick asked.

The girls shook their heads. "I'll go ring him on the intercom," Mick volunteered.

"Do you have to tell Frank right this second?" Stevie asked. "Carole will probably have her back in no time."

Mick wavered. "Well, I guess we could wait a couple of minutes. But that's it. A loose horse is a loose horse. And with this storm coming . . ."

"He's right," said Kate. "If Carole doesn't get her back right away, Dad's got to know."

"Maybe I should go help her—" Lisa started to say.

"No! Nobody else is wandering off," John declared. "Carole shouldn't have gone by herself. Where did she head?"

"We don't know," Kate said. The five of them stared outside, but visibility was bad. They couldn't see more than twenty feet. Carole had literally disappeared.

"Darn! I hope she remembers how huge the property is," John said worriedly.

The group walked to the tack room, where they passed an anxious quarter of an hour. Mick and John had chores to do, but they didn't want to leave until Carole was back safely. When she burst in, everyone jumped up in relief.

"You got her, right?" Stevie asked with confidence.

"I need a saddle and bridle," Carole said breathlessly. "I got halfway to the end of the pasture before I lost the tracks. It's coming down hard and I'll make better time on horseback. Will you hand me that bridle?"

Slowly John started shaking his head. "No," he said quietly.

"I thought I could take Stewball. He's good at—" Carole stopped and looked at John. "No?" she repeated. "Is that what you said?"

"Yes. I mean, yes, I said no. You're not going back out there, Carole."

"But I have to!" Carole protested, her voice bordering on hysterical. "It's my fault that she escaped, and I have to get her back or—"

John put a steadying hand on her shoulder. "First of all, it's not your fault. You bolted the door, didn't you?"

Carole nodded. "I'm sure I did."

"Well, then—"

"But, you see, I should have stayed with her instead of going and riding those other horses because I knew she was scared and—"

"Carole," John interrupted, "it's not your fault. Anyway, it wouldn't matter if it *was*. It will be dark in an hour. It's snowing like crazy. Going to look for the mare now would be the most idiotic thing you could do."

"But—"

"No buts," John said firmly.

Stevie, Kate, and Lisa looked from John to Carole and back. They knew John was right, but they felt awful for Carole. They knew she had formed an instant attachment to the mare. When Mick left to tell Frank, Lisa put a consoling arm around Carole. "They'll find her in the morning. She won't go far."

"The *morning?*" Carole whispered, dismayed. She could have kicked herself for not staying with the mare. Why had she gone and ridden the other horses? She had let down one beautiful black horse already, and look what

51

had happened to him. Her eyes filling with tears, Carole looked out the window. The few flakes had escalated into a real storm. "If anything happens to her out there, I'll never forgive myself!" she vowed.

THAT EVENING THE mood in the bunkhouse was glum. Carole headed for bed right after dinner. Not wanting to disturb her, Stevie and Lisa followed suit. Now they couldn't sleep. They could hear Carole sniffling every few minutes. It was torture! Finally Lisa had to say something. "Carole, are you okay?" she whispered across the room.

Carole gulped, trying to make her voice sound calm. "Oh, yeah, I'm fine," she said. Normally she would have talked things over with The Saddle Club, but this time she didn't know what to say. Everyone would think she was getting too involved, making too much of it. She sighed aloud. That was the problem with The Saddle Club: Sometimes they cared too much.

Carole tried to look on the bright side. Frank had been very understanding. Several times he had told her that it wasn't her fault, that they ought to have replaced that bolt months ago. And he had organized a search party for the morning. She had to believe they would find the mare and bring her back. And yet, Carole wondered, why didn't that thought make her happier?

THE NEXT MORNING, Carole was awake at dawn. She had tossed and turned all night. She wasn't sure she had slept even one wink. A glance out the window told her that it had stopped snowing, at least for now. As fast as she could, she yanked on long underwear, jeans, two shirts, a big bulky sweater, boots, gloves, a scarf, and a hat. She raced through the fresh snow to the main barn. Maybe there would be news about the mare. Maybe she had come home in the night of her own accord.

The first person Carole saw was Walter Brightstar, John's father and the ranch's head wrangler. He greeted her warmly.

"I was down mending fence in the big pasture all day, so I didn't get to say hello yesterday," he explained.

But Carole heard only three words. "The big pasture?" she said. "Did you see a black mare go by—loose—in the afternoon?"

Walter shook his head regretfully. "John already asked me. Can't say that I did. But that pasture is huge. She might have walked right by me, ten yards away. With the snow, I wouldn't have noticed. If I were her, though, I would have headed north."

"North?" said Carole, paying careful attention. "Why north?"

"That's where she came from. If she's trying to get back home, that's the direction."

Carole nodded. She had several more questions. "Are you going out with the search party? When do they leave? Can I take Stewball? Stevie reminded me how good he is on the trail."

Walter began doubtfully, "No, I'm not going. I've got work here. And sure, sure, you can take Stewball. But you'd better hurry. They're leaving in two minutes!"

Carole was down the aisle and into the tack room before the words were out of Walter's mouth. Frank was inside, dressed for riding. Begging him to wait, Carole reached for a set of tack.

"Carole, I—"

"Please, please, I'll only be two minutes, I promise!"

Frank frowned. "It's not that. I don't mind waiting. It's just . . . well, I'm not sure you should go. John and I are all set and we both know this country well. It could be a very long day—cold, exhausting. I don't know *how* long because I don't know how far this silly mare has gotten herself."

Carole waited in silence, trying not to cry. She *had* to go. It had never entered her mind that she couldn't. She felt Frank studying her face. A moment later he relented.

"Well, okay, if it means that much to you—"

Carole didn't wait for him to change his mind. She saddled Stewball in seconds flat. "I know, boy, you're expecting Stevie, but I need your herding and roundup skills out there today. We've got to find one of your stablemates who's lost out there." Carole took a quick glance out the window. It was partly sunny, but more snow was expected that night. She shivered a little as she tightened Stewball's cinch and led the pinto outside.

Lisa, Stevie, Kate, and Phyllis all came out to see them

54

off. Stevie gave Stewball a pat and told him to take care of Carole. Phyllis gave Frank bottled water, a Thermos of hot coffee, and a backpack of sandwiches, which he tied into his saddlebag.

"We expect you back by noon," she said brightly.

Frank leaned down to kiss his wife. "At the latest," he promised.

As the three of them set off, John turned around in his saddle. He smiled and waved good-bye to Lisa. Lisa caught his eye. She blushed. She had been imagining what it would have been like if John had kissed her good-bye—

"Yee-haw, it's pie time!" Stevie hollered.

Lisa gave her a withering glance. "Thanks," she said. "You really know how to wreck a moment."

"A moment? What moment?" Stevie followed Lisa inside, frowning in confusion.

"Oh, you know," Lisa murmured, her eyes far away. "It's so romantic when someone leaves, saying good-bye and everything . . ." She sighed. They were in the foyer hanging up their coats and trading wet boots for moccasins and slippers.

Stevie gave her friend a disgusted look. "Have you been watching too many B Westerns, Lisa? Leaving isn't romantic. What's romantic about not seeing a person? *Arriving*, on the other hand . . ."

IT WAS THE perfect day to make pies: freezing cold! The girls wished Carole, Frank, and John could have been at home with them. But the three were expert riders. They would never do anything unsafe. "Just think of it as a long winter trail ride," Kate suggested when they were gathered in the warm, brightly lit kitchen.

"Yeah. With most people I'd laugh, but Carole's crazy enough to want to go riding on a day like this," Stevie said.

Lisa agreed. "If she didn't have to go find the black mare, she'd be on our cases all day to go for a pleasure ride!"

As the girls watched, Phyllis set out flour and sugar. She preheated the oven to 350 degrees. "We'll try apple pie today," she announced. "As I said before, a good crust is the secret of a good pie. The filling is easy: You just mix up fruit, sugar, and spices—whatever's in season—"

"Except for mincemeat pie," Stevie interrupted. "That's got real beef in it, doesn't it?"

Phyllis laughed. "In the old days it did. And you can probably still find recipes lying around for *real* mincemeat. But when people serve mincemeat at Thanksgiving or Christmas, it's just nuts, raisins, sugar, and spices. It has a meaty flavor, but there's no meat in there."

Lisa stared at her. "You mean all these years I've been refusing my grandmother's mincemeat for no reason? I always thought it sounded *disgusting*, so I stuck to my mother's pumpkin and pecan."

"You'll have to try it next year," Phyllis said. "It's one of my favorites." While they were chatting, Kate's mother scooped cups of flour from a large canister. She showed the girls how to level the top with a knife to get an exact measurement. Then she gestured for them to do the same. "It's no good if I cook and you watch, because you won't really learn till you try it yourselves—and try it again and again. So each of us is going to make two or three pies," she explained. "We're lucky: The ranch kitchen is semi-industrial, meaning that it's set up to produce dinner for fifty. Everyone can have her own measuring cups, mixing bowls, pie plates, et cetera. How's that filling coming, Kate?"

Kate groaned. "I always forget how long it takes to peel enough apples for even one pie. My hands are killing me."

"It's good exercise," Phyllis said briskly.

Stevie and Lisa smiled at one another. The older Devines were no-nonsense parents. They believed that children should work hard and play hard. It was one of the reasons the ranch was so much fun: Everyone was expected to take part in the chores, whether it was mucking stalls or peeling apples. But then everyone joined in the celebrations, too. Kate rolled her eyes good-naturedly and picked up another apple.

"Don't you want to have the butter out getting soft?" Lisa inquired. She remembered that rule from making chocolate-chip cookies. It was easier to cream the butter and sugar if the butter had softened somewhat.

Phyllis shook her head. "No. Butter for a crust should be hard and chilled. Otherwise you'll have trouble cutting it into the flour. If it's warm and soft, it mushes into the flour, and it doesn't create the texture you want."

"What is *cutting*, anyway?" Stevie inquired. "It sounds like you take a knife and hack up the butter."

"You do, sort of," Phyllis said. "Although nowadays we can be a bit more sophisticated." She first demonstrated the most basic cutting technique: slicing pieces of cold butter into the flour with two knives. "But there's also a tool specifically intended for this task." Phyllis reached into a drawer and held up a wooden-handled pastry blender. She demonstrated how to use the implement. "You see? It's almost like having six knives cutting at the same time."

"So that's what that is!" Stevie exclaimed. "My mom let my brothers and me use it with modeling dough, so I thought it was a—a modeling dough blender!"

Kate flicked an apple peel at Stevie. "Ha-ha."

"Ha-ha yourself!" Stevie shot back.

One thing is sure, Lisa thought, eyeing her two friends, *with Stevie in the kitchen, we won't lack for entertainment.*

"Here, I'll give it a try," Lisa volunteered.

"Great," said Phyllis.

Starting tentatively, Lisa began to cut her flour and butter. Soon she was mimicking Phyllis's deft movements. The recipe said the flour and butter should "resemble coarse meal." Lisa had no idea what coarse meal looked like, but pretty soon Phyllis stopped her. "Perfect. You see how the ingredients are mixed? They're not pastelike or gluey, which happens if you overmix them. Excellent job, Lisa."

Lisa glowed. It was such a little thing, but with Kate's mother as her teacher, she already felt more confident in the kitchen. Phyllis had a relaxed style that made her a natural teacher. Lisa's own mother was, like her daughter, a perfectionist. Mrs. Atwood kept the kitchen spotless, even *while* she was baking or making dinner. If she spilled anything—water, sugar, coffee grounds—she wiped it up that instant. And the Atwoods' kitchen was so organized that it got on Lisa's nerves. Yes, it was true that staples like flour and sugar were kept in labeled glass jars. But Lisa didn't like to disturb them. She was always afraid she would spill something or make a mistake, like getting brown sugar mixed with white. That kind of thing drove her mother crazy. Lisa said as much to the group in the kitchen.

Phyllis nodded sympathetically. "Kate's grandmother, my mother, was like that. She was a marvelous cook—still is, in fact. But I never felt free to experiment in the kitchen at home. I didn't really learn to cook until I got to college. I've never worried about cooking for the guests, not even when we had the crew from Hollywood staying with us." Phyllis laughed. "But when Mom comes for Thanksgiving or Christmas, I stay up half the night getting ready!"

"It's true," Kate said, grinning. "You've never seen a woman go from calm to panic so fast."

Stevie and Lisa chuckled. Neither of them could imagine Kate's mother worrying about her cooking. "How's this?" Stevie asked, holding up her mixing bowl. "I did mine by the old method of two knives."

Phyllis examined the mixture. "Not quite done."

Stevie's face fell. In spite of herself, she was feeling competitive with Lisa.

"But don't worry," Phyllis hurried on, "because I haven't even showed you the best method."

"You haven't?" Stevie and Lisa said in unison.

Phyllis shook her head. "Nope. It's right over there." They looked to see where she was pointing.

"A food processor!" Lisa exclaimed, scandalized. "But I thought with cooking and baking you had to do everything from scratch, and by hand, or else you were cheating!"

Phyllis raised her eyebrows. "A nice idea. Actually, the more you can cheat, the better. And now I'll show you how to make perfect, instant crust with a flick of the On-Off button."

In a matter of seconds, Phyllis had used the electric food processor to mix the flour and butter. Then she moved on to the next step: adding tablespoonfuls of ice water so that the crust would stick together. A quick pulse of the machine and the dough was ready to be gathered into a ball. "Now we'll let it chill for an hour. Meanwhile, you can both try the 'cheating' method. I'll help my poor, overworked daughter peel apples."

Before the girls could trade places with Phyllis, there was a loud knock on the front door. "I'll get it!" Kate cried, tossing the peeler aside. She ran out of the kitchen. A moment later she was back. "Company!" she announced.

The girls turned to see their old friend Christine Lonetree in the doorway.

"Christine!" cried Stevie and Lisa. They ran to embrace her. Christine was a close friend of the Devines and, like Kate, was an out-of-town member of The Saddle Club. She lived close enough to the Bar None to ride over, and often did, on her horse, Arrow.

"I was out on Arrow when I remembered you guys were here on a visit. So I stuck him in an empty stall and stopped in."

"We're so glad you did, Christine," said Phyllis.

"How is it out there?" Lisa asked anxiously.

Christine shivered. "It's cold—and I mean *cold*," she said. "It's a good thing I ride bareback. Arrow has better circulation than I do and he keeps me warm."

That was not the weather report Lisa had hoped for. Quickly the girls explained the situation with the black mare to Christine. "Gosh, I didn't see any sign of a loose horse."

Phyllis looked at the clock. "They've been out a couple of hours already," she noted. Then her face brightened.

"Listen, Christine, why don't you help us make pies and stay for dinner tonight? We'd love your company."

Christine had barely said yes when Kate thrust a paring knife into her hand. "Peel," she ordered. "Peel, peel, peel, peel, peel."

6

CAROLE WILLED HERSELF to ride on in silence. She had begged to come, despite Frank's warnings. She couldn't start complaining now. It seemed colder than when they had started six hours earlier. The sun had come out briefly, then vanished behind clouds. Carole wriggled her toes in her boots to make sure they were still there. She held the reins loosely, giving Stewball his head to follow the other two horses. The cold seemed to press in on them. There was still no sign of the black mare.

Up ahead, Frank suddenly reined in his bay. "We're coming to a split in the trail," he announced. "We've got to make a decision."

Beside him John shook his head. "I just don't understand it," he said. "I was sure my dad would be right."

"So did I, John," Frank answered.

"Why would the mare run away if not to go back home—where she came from?" John mused aloud. "And yet we've ridden north, northeast, and northwest without seeing a single hoofprint."

"It sure beats me how any horse . . ."

Carole half listened to the conversation. *If only I knew where you were!* she thought. Beneath her, Stewball shifted uneasily. The pinto seemed impatient to turn around. He had been trying to go in the opposite direction for a couple of hours at least. "There's nothing over there, boy," Carole murmured. "Nothing but desert and wide-open stretches and a handful of wild horses. You're not going to find—" Midthought, Carole stopped. A lightbulb turned on in her brain. She clapped a hand to her mouth.

"I just thought of something!" she exclaimed, bursting into Frank and John's discussion. "The wild horses! That's it! I'll bet the black mare went to join the wild herd!"

John's eyes lit up. "Carole, I think you've got it!"

As everyone at the Bar None knew, herds of wild horses ran free on the federal property that surrounded the ranch, and sometimes on the ranch itself. Kate's horse, Moonglow, had come from one of those herds. Kate had adopted the mare as part of a government program that kept the herds small enough so that they could survive. Most of the time the horses were left alone to graze and forage on the range. It was easy to forget they even existed.

Frank frowned. "You could be right. But why would a tame horse go wild?"

Carole opened her mouth to reply. Then she shut it just as fast. There was no way of explaining it. How could she say, "I just know she's there. I know it the way I know two plus two is four," and expect anyone to believe her? She felt John's eyes on her.

"It's—It's just a thought," she said. "But Stewball seems to want to head in that direction. That is, if the horses still stick to the area around the base of the mountain."

John spoke up. "They do, Carole. I saw them there last month."

"Could we at least check?" Carole asked, her fingers crossed. "It's worth a try, isn't it?"

Frank looked off into the distance. "That's a long trek through the snow," he said doubtfully. He sighed. "I like the looks of that mare, and I'd hate to lose her right after we bought her, but three people are a lot more important than one horse."

Carole knew Frank was right, and that he had to take responsibility for them. But if it were up to her, she'd risk anything to get the mare back . . .

"I think we ought to give it a shot, boss," said John. "We're not starving out here—or freezing." He chuckled. "At least, not yet, we're not. I, for one, can put up with a little more discomfort if it means bringing the mare

65

home." Something in the way he spoke made Carole feel that John understood she was going on intuition, and that he trusted her intuition.

Frank squinted up at the sky. He checked the sandwich supply in his saddlebag. He studied John's and Carole's faces. Finally he said, "We'll give it three more hours total, including the hour it's going to take us to get home. If we wrap around the mountain from here, we may catch the herd on the way back. If we don't, the black mare is going to have to come in out of the cold of her own accord."

Carole shivered again, and this time not from the cold. As they started off in the opposite direction, she caught John Brightstar's eye. "Thank you," she mouthed.

"No problem," he mouthed back, giving her a thumbs-up.

Stewball was pleased. Without waiting for a cue, he picked up his pace, from a lagging shuffle to a swinging walk. It was as if he wanted to tell them they had made the right decision. Carole felt her spirits rising. She had been in a daze all morning. She'd almost *known* that their search was going to be fruitless. Now she felt optimistic.

"Hey, let's sing a little to keep our spirits up," John suggested.

"Great idea," said Carole.

John started with "I've Been Working on the Railroad." Carole chimed in, then went on with "Erie Canal."

"Hey, you're not going to forget 'Home on the Range,' are you?" Frank demanded.

Carole sat up straighter in the saddle. She lifted her hand off the saddle horn where it had been resting and reined Stewball properly. Singing "Home on the Range" when you *were* on the range was a thrill and a privilege— and it was a moment Carole would never forget. She didn't want to spoil it by slouching!

The singing was fun, and what was more, Carole thought, it got them breathing deeply, which helped their circulation. Before she knew it, close to an hour had passed. They were approaching the valley sandwiched between the mountain and Two-Mile Creek. The creek was completely frozen. Luckily they didn't have to cross it. Instead they wandered alongside it. They automatically fell silent so as not to scare the horses if they were nearby.

They didn't have to wait long to find out. Rounding a large patch of shrub bush, Carole caught her breath. The black mare was standing about fifty yards away. Carole felt her heart soar as she caught sight of Cobalt's twin. She was struck for a second time by the uncanny similarities. She didn't trust herself to speak. And it wasn't just the mare's resemblance to the stallion that took Carole's breath away. It was her solitude in the wilderness, and her beauty—night black against white, unspoiled snow.

"She almost looks as if she's been waiting for us," John murmured.

Carole frowned. "But where's the rest of the herd?" It seemed strange that the mare would have separated from them.

Frank gestured toward the mountain trail. "They probably caught our scent and took off," he said. "I'd put money on it."

Just then a high, distant whinny pierced the air.

"It's the stallion!" John whispered, pointing. "He's telling her to come with them." The three riders craned their necks to catch a glimpse of the herd, but they were too late. The horses had vanished into the gray afternoon, leaving only a trail of hoofprints.

The mare pricked her ears. She turned her elegant head toward the mountain. A moment later she answered the stallion's whinny. But she didn't move. She seemed to be hesitating, wondering which way to go.

"You two cut left and right in case she runs," Frank said quietly. "I've got my lasso ready."

Carole started in the saddle. She had been so caught up in the scene, she hadn't been at all prepared for Frank's order. Obviously, though, that was what they had come for. Fortunately Stewball seemed to know what to do without being told. He jogged left, flanking the mare, as John guided Tex to the right. In a matter of seconds, Frank was close enough to swing his rope. It whistled through the air. Carole fought an instinct to yell, to scare the mare off. The lasso landed neatly around the black neck.

Carole felt herself cringe. The mare had looked so beautiful standing alone in the wilderness. Now she was just another horse in captivity.

Don't be silly, Carole told herself angrily. *You didn't ride seven hours not to catch her!*

"Carole, why don't you hop down and halter her?" Frank suggested. "She must have lost hers out here somewhere."

Carole jumped off Stewball and took the halter Frank handed her. She could tell the mare was ready to run. Her ears swiveled back and forth. She seemed to be waiting for a sign. For a moment Carole stood stock-still. The mare raised her head warily. *She's poised between captivity and the wild*, Carole thought, *and it's up to me to help her choose captivity*.

"Here, girl," John said from aboard Tex. "Come on, we just want to take you home."

Turning his horse to face the mare directly, Frank clucked encouragingly through his teeth.

The mare paid them no heed. She stayed focused on Carole, who began to approach her at a snail's pace. The closer Carole got, the more undecided the mare seemed. Carole spoke soothingly to her. She kept the halter behind her back so that it wouldn't scare the mare. When Carole was close enough to touch her, the mare looked over her shoulder a final time. Then she blew through her nostrils and lowered her head. She almost seemed to be sighing. Carole encircled her neck with an arm and slipped the halter on. "Good girl," she breathed. "What a good girl." She took a lead shank from her pocket and clipped it to the halter. Now the mare was ready to be ponied home behind Stewball. Carole remounted, keeping the lead in her free hand.

Frank was clearly very pleased. "A happy ending," he declared. "Nice work, Carole, John. Let's head for home. I'll bet my wife's got something in the oven!"

Nobody talked much on the way back. They were all cold and tired. But it wasn't just physical discomfort that was bothering Carole. It was strange, but now she almost wished she hadn't said anything about the wild horses. She felt like a traitor to the black mare. Most horses escaped from their stalls because they were bored, or because they wanted something on the other side—because the grass was greener. But Carole was convinced that the mare had run away to be free.

But if I hadn't said anything, we wouldn't have found her, and she might not have been able to survive the winter out here, she reasoned. She glanced back at the mare. The horse wasn't making any fuss. She was walking and jogging behind Stewball as calm as could be.

When they neared the ranch, John broke the silence with a question to Frank. "How much is known about the mare's history?"

"Not a heck of a lot," Frank admitted. "I do know that the other four are more experienced. I took her as part of a package deal. The trader who sold them to me had only had her for a few weeks. Poor girl's probably confused. She'll settle in when she realizes that the Bar None is going to be her permanent home. This moving around is never good for a horse."

If only it were just that! Carole thought. She said a silent prayer that maybe, just maybe, the mare was glad they had caught her.

"I SEE THEM!" Stevie shrieked. She had been staring out the kitchen window for so long she could hardly believe it when the riders came into view.

"Yay," said Christine.

"Are you sure?" Kate asked, running to join her.

"Look! There's Stewball and Carole in front, and they've got the mare! Bet you anything that crazy pinto found her!" Stevie boasted. She was as proud of Stewball as if she'd owned and trained him herself.

The girls yanked on jackets and ran out to greet Carole, Frank, and John. "Don't you want to come?" Lisa called to Phyllis.

"I can't!" Phyllis replied. "Somebody's got to watch the pies!"

The girls had put off baking two of the pies, hoping that the roundup posse would make it back in time to try some hot. Pie would be just the thing for a late-afternoon snack.

Lisa shook her head ruefully. "Boy, I sure don't have a cook's instincts. I would have forgotten all about them," she said, sprinting for the door.

Outside the barn, the three were dismounting wearily.

71

Stevie, Lisa, Christine, and Kate walked toward the black mare to welcome her home.

As they approached, the mare wheeled around. She laid her ears back and bared her teeth. Carole didn't notice right away. She was loosening Stewball's cinch with her free hand. The mare strained at the end of her lead shank. All at once she pulled free. Her eyes rolling wildly, she reared, then shied away.

"Grab her!" Frank called.

Stevie lunged for the lead shank but missed.

"No! Let me," Carole ordered. Instinct took over. She walked slowly toward the mare. She breathed in and out, in and out, willing the mare to sense the calming rhythm. She whispered nonsense words. Everyone watched as the mare stopped and listened to Carole. Carole inched closer. She reached out and stroked the mare's shoulder. Then she unclipped the lead line. She put it into her pocket. She knew she wouldn't need it. "Come on, girl, we're home now." The mare's head drooped slightly. She followed Carole into the barn.

Frank, John, and the four girls stared at the retreating pair. They couldn't believe what they had seen. It was so strange, and so special, that nobody wanted to talk about it. So nobody did.

A LITTLE NERVOUSLY, Lisa removed a pie from the oven and brought it to the table. Stevie was right beside her with *her* pie. "Ta-*dah!*" Lisa said.

Everyone burst into applause. "You might want to wait until you've tried some before you clap," Lisa remarked.

"I don't need to. I can tell from the smell," John said.

"And I can tell from the other two pies we ate waiting around for you guys," Stevie joked.

"Do you want to do the honors, girls, or should I?" Frank inquired.

"Please, be my guest," Lisa said with a grin. She handed him a knife and a pie server. Frank sliced and served with gusto, first one pie, then the other, until everyone had a piece. Lisa insisted on having a smaller piece than everyone else, but she did take one. They all dug in.

"Perfect," said Christine. "Just perfect."

At the look on John's face, Lisa felt a rush of pride. When he asked for another sliver a few minutes later, she was even more thrilled. Now she knew why her mother liked it so much when people asked for seconds. It was a compliment, pure and simple. Lisa could hardly wait for the big dinner she and Stevie were going to make.

"Are you sure my wife didn't make these?" Frank asked, a merry light in his eyes. "They taste suspiciously like hers. Suspiciously *good*," he added.

Phyllis shook her head. "I didn't touch them! All I did was demonstrate, right, girls?"

"Right, Mom," Lisa joked. Out at the Bar None, it did feel as if Phyllis were their surrogate mother—except that she didn't interfere the way their own moms did!

As they ate, Frank filled everyone in on the search and rescue mission. "It was Carole's idea to look in the valley where the herd congregates," he said. "That was very smart thinking."

"How'd you think of that, Carole?" Stevie asked, impressed as always by Carole's horsey intuition.

"I—I don't know," Carole said, flustered.

Too late Stevie realized that Carole didn't want the spotlight on her. The attention seemed to make her uncomfortable. Quickly Stevie changed the subject back to the pies. "I guess now my only problem is going to be what kind to make. There are so many great pies: blueberry, strawberry-rhubarb, lemon meringue . . ."

Phyllis smiled. "And now that you know how to make crust, you can also make quiches, potpies—"

Stevie gulped down her mouthful. "Wait a minute. Did you say *potpies*? Do you mean to tell me that I, Stevie Lake, am now capable of making, say, a *chicken potpie*?"

Phyllis nodded.

Stevie pretended to swoon. "I have no further ambitions in life!" she cried.

As soon as she could, Carole sneaked out to the barn. Or not exactly *sneaked*. She slipped away quietly so that no one would follow her. Dinner had been pushed back to eight o'clock because everyone had eaten so much pie. Carole figured that gave her a few hours with the black mare.

Frank had instructed Carole to put the mare in a stall that night—one that had a double bolt. The mare hardly seemed to have moved at all. The bedding in her stall was barely mussed. She stood by the door, her ears pricked and straining.

"You belong out there, don't you, girl?" Carole murmured.

"How is she doing?" said a voice down the aisle.

Her heart pounding, Carole spun around to see Frank. She hadn't counted on his being there. But, of course, after a day away from the horses, Frank would want to give the place a once-over to make sure everything was ship-shape. Carole didn't know why, but she felt as if she'd been caught doing something wrong. Her hands felt sweaty.

Aloud she said, "I don't know. She still seems kind of nervous."

Frank joined her at the stall and looked in. "Hmmm . . . You're right. Today was pretty exciting for her." He glanced thoughtfully at Carole. "Maybe we ought to assign you to the black mare as a special project. She seems to trust you more than anyone. If you could work with her, help her settle in, I'd be grateful. How would you feel about that, Carole?"

"I'd feel . . . fine!" Carole said, an understatement if there ever was one.

"Great. Wonderful. I want to try her under saddle just as soon as you think she's ready. And keep me informed of her progress." Frank turned to go.

"Um, Frank . . . ," Carole started. She had no idea what she was going to say. But whatever it was, this might be her only chance.

"Yes?"

Carole took a deep breath. "I—I know this might sound crazy, but to be honest, I think the mare would be happier"—she steeled herself—"where we found her today." Now that she had said it, she felt sick with apprehension about how Frank would react. Who was she to tell him how to run his stable?

"Go on," said Frank. To Carole's relief, he leaned against the stall door, indicating that he would listen to what she had to say.

Carole started to talk. She had nothing prepared. She just went with her gut. Everything came out in a rush. "It's just—I—I have a strong feeling that this horse belongs in the wild. She doesn't seem comfortable with people. And the way she ran away to find the herd— Maybe *she* was one of those wild horses, too. Maybe she got rounded up from a herd somewhere, for one of the government sales, and—and didn't adjust to life in captivity." Carole paused to catch her breath. "Maybe she never will." She hadn't intended to say all that. She hadn't even formulated that specific theory until then. But everything she had noticed seemed to fall into place.

Frank waited a moment, his lips pursed in thought. When he spoke, his tone was matter-of-fact. "I hear what you're saying, Carole. And you could be right. You could very well be right. But that doesn't change one simple fact. This mare is an investment. I bought her to use on the ranch. And that's what I'm going to do with her."

At Frank's words, Carole felt tears spring to her eyes. She clenched her fists so that she wouldn't cry.

"Now, we haven't tried her under saddle yet. But the dealer assured me that all the horses were broken."

"But—" Carole began.

Frank held up a finger. Carole swallowed. She wanted to say that the horse might be broken all right, but that didn't necessarily mean she was rideable. Anybody could slap a bridle and saddle on a horse and call it trained.

"I know it may sound harsh to you to think of a horse as money spent or money to be earned," Frank continued. "If it's any consolation, I've had this conversation with Kate many a time. Unfortunately, that's how you run a ranch. I have no doubt this mare will come around. Especially with you to help. We've just got to think positively. You'll still work with her, won't you?"

Carole nodded miserably. "Yes, of course," she said, her voice threatening to crack. "I'd love to." She made an effort to smile. She didn't want to be a baby about this! But at the back of her mind, the barest hint of a plan was forming . . .

THE NEXT MORNING dawned bright and bitter cold. Kate, John, Lisa, and Stevie climbed into the ranch van. They were off to town to do some shopping for the Devines. Nobody had the heart to wake Carole.

"She must be exhausted from yesterday," Kate said.

"I'll say. And she was tossing and turning all night," commented Stevie.

Lisa raised her eyebrows. "Do you think it's the mare?"

Stevie nodded.

"But she's back safe and sound," said John. "Why should Carole worry?"

Stevie and Lisa exchanged glances. Taking turns, they

told Kate and John the story of Cobalt. "And the black mare looks exactly like him," Lisa finished.

"I still don't get what the problem is," John said. He turned out of the long ranch driveway and onto the one road that led into town.

"There is no problem—yet," Stevie said.

"It's just that Carole's gotten pretty attached to the mare already," Lisa explained.

"And the mare seems to be getting pretty attached to her," Kate added speculatively.

"Carole does have a way with her," John agreed.

"We just don't want her to get, you know, overly involved," Stevie concluded.

"Sounds to me like you guys are getting overly involved," John remarked, his eyes on the road.

The girls exchanged glances. They were all thinking the same thing: What a typical thing for a guy to say. It wasn't even worth a response.

WHEN THEY GOT to town, Kate and John headed for the hardware store, leaving Stevie and Lisa to tackle the grocery list.

"Meet back in an hour?" asked Kate.

"Sounds good," Stevie answered.

John took Lisa aside for a second. "Maybe you should get some more apples," he suggested.

"They're not on the list, but sure, why not? Everyone likes apples," Lisa said.

"I meant so that you could make some more of that pie," John explained. "You know what they say about the way to a man's heart . . ." He grinned.

Lisa felt herself blushing. "I'll try to remember," she said.

"FIRST ITEM ON the list: condensed milk," Stevie read. They were standing in the fruits and vegetables aisle of the Super-Shop. "Wait. *Condensed* milk? What do you think that is?"

Lisa looked over Stevie's shoulder at the list. "Weird. I have no idea. I guess we should go look in dairy, though."

They trooped to the end of the aisle. "Skim milk, one percent, two percent, whole, organic skim, organic whole, lactose aid, skim plus . . . Gee, they have every kind *but* condensed," Lisa said.

Stevie picked up several cartons and inspected them. "Maybe regular milk would be okay."

Lisa wasn't so sure. If there was one thing she had learned in home ec, it was that beginning cooks should stick to recipes. Somehow she had a feeling that beginning shoppers should stick to lists.

"Oh, I bet I know what Phyllis means!" Stevie said suddenly. "She probably wants the little pints of milk for putting into the guests' lunches."

Lisa smiled. "Brilliant. That's got to be it. How many should we get?" She started tossing pints of whole milk into their cart.

"At least four. There are four guests, aren't there?"

"Yeah, so we'd better get eight to be safe. My mom always says it's better to get a couple extra rather than go short. And eight will take care of two lunches," Lisa pointed out. "Okay, let's see. What's next? Pastry and flour."

"Pastry? That's *all* it says?"

Lisa held out the list. "Yeah, see?"

This, thought Stevie, was total insanity. "But—But what kind does she want? I mean, you can't just say *pastry* when there's doughnuts, danishes, turnovers—"

"It must be for dessert. Why don't you go to the bakery and see what they have? Get a couple of each."

Stevie was more than happy to oblige. Bakery sections usually had samples. It took her all of about ten seconds to spot the tray of goodies. She paused, planning her attack. Then, with a quick glance right and left, she went into action. First she walked nonchalantly by and picked up a broken cookie. It was gone in one bite. Then she furrowed her brow and pretended to think hard. "Pastries . . . What a great idea," she said aloud. She went up to the counter and ordered several. The woman began packing them into a white bakery box.

"Oh, what are these? Free samples?" Stevie asked loudly, looking at the tray as if she'd just noticed it.

"Yes, help yourself," the woman said. Stevie nabbed a brownie piece and a petit four. The petit four tasted disgusting. Stevie felt gypped—and entitled to another sample. The woman's back was turned. Stevie shoved a minimuffin into her mouth. The woman turned around.

"Would you mind if I had a second sample? They're so good," Stevie said, her mouth full.

The woman gave Stevie an odd look. "Please go ahead," she said, staring at the muffin crumbs on Stevie's chin.

"Thanks, I will." Stevie took the last remaining brownie piece. She deliberated for a moment. "You know, I ought to get one for the road, too!"

Before the woman could protest, Stevie had grabbed the bakery box off the counter and another half cookie. "Thanks again!" she called, sprinting toward frozen foods.

She ran smack-dab into Lisa.

"Mission accomplished. Four eclairs, two brownies, two blondies, and assorted Italian cookies."

Lisa grinned. "Is that what you ate or what you bought?" she asked.

"Who, me?" Stevie said innocently.

Lisa rolled her eyes. "Come on, let's go find the spices."

"What do we need?" Stevie asked when they were standing in front of the display.

"You're not going to believe this, but we need all of them."

"All of them?" Stevie demanded. "Are you sure?"

"Look. It says 'all spice.' Do you think Phyllis wants to update her spice rack?"

Stevie shrugged. "Could be. But I think it's strange. In fact, the whole list is weird."

Lisa agreed. "It is weird. Maybe she didn't want to explain things to us because, I don't know, she thought we'd be offended."

"Boy, I sure wouldn't have been," Stevie said. "The more explanation, the better. But you're probably right."

"I just can't see us getting one of *every* spice," Lisa said worriedly.

"Yeah. Let's just get the most common ones, like cinnamon and nutmeg."

Lisa smiled with relief. "That's a great idea."

A few minutes later they were done. Lisa glanced at her watch. "Ohmigosh! We only have five minutes to meet Kate and John!" she exclaimed.

"Don't worry, we're almost finished." Stevie grabbed the list. "I'll go get the chicken, you get the crushed tomatoes, and I'll meet you in line."

The two of them split up and dashed to their respective sections. Lisa couldn't find any truly crushed tomatoes, but she got the most bruised ones available. Phyllis hadn't indicated what kind of chicken, so Stevie got her favorite: breaded chicken patties. They were back in the checkout line in minutes.

"Are you sure we got everything?" Lisa asked. She took the list back and mentally checked off their purchases. Out of the corner of her eye she saw a look of horror dawn on Stevie's face. "What? What is it?"

Stevie pointed wordlessly to the list.

"I know," Lisa said. "I'm checking to make sure—"

Stevie was shaking her head, still pointing. All at once, Lisa got her meaning. She turned the list over. There were at least another fifteen items on the back. Lisa groaned. Stevie beat her hand against her forehead. A couple of shoppers turned around to look at them. They didn't care. Together they grabbed the cart—and ran.

8

CAROLE WOKE UP to the midday sun streaming through the bunkhouse window. She yawned and shifted groggily in her bed. Then she sat bolt upright. The clock on the wall said half past twelve! She had slept nearly fifteen hours! That meant that nobody had been there in the morning to let the black mare out of her stall or greet her or tell her it was going to be all right. Not wanting to lose another minute, Carole thrust the wool blankets back and slipped out of her sleeping bag.

As she brushed her teeth, Carole realized she was being a little unfair. *Somebody* would have greeted the mare and fed her and turned her out—whether it was John or Walter or Mick or one of the other wranglers of The Saddle Club or Frank himself. But Carole was sure the black mare would be afraid until she saw the only human she trusted. "I'm coming, girl," she said aloud. "Don't worry, I'm coming."

On the way to the barn, Carole saw Phyllis heading to the main house. She put up a hand but didn't stop. Phyllis, however, had other ideas. "You've got to eat something, Carole," she insisted. "After yesterday's ride? Absolutely, positively, no ifs, ands, or buts. Come on in the house. I'll fix you some brunch."

Carole wavered. She really had no choice but to do as Phyllis said. She noticed that Phyllis's voice sounded odd.

"I think I'm coming down with something," Phyllis admitted when Carole asked her about it in the kitchen. "Nothing big, just a winter cold. You be careful yourself or you'll get it, too."

"Can I do anything?" Carole asked.

Phyllis thought for a minute. "Would you mind running up to the attic and grabbing the hot-water bottle? I think I'll fill it and take a nap."

Anxiously Carole went to do the errand. She wanted to get out to the barn as soon as possible. But of course, anything she could do for Phyllis, she would. Up in the attic, it was hard to see. She couldn't find the light switch, and it took her several minutes to locate the bottle.

"Thanks a million," said Phyllis when she returned. "Now, here, eat your cereal and toast."

Sick with worry, Carole gulped down a bowl of oatmeal and a piece of toast. She was about to excuse herself when she heard the gang clattering in.

"Oh, good," Phyllis said. "Everybody's back from town. They'll keep you company. Gang! Carole's up and she's in here!"

As Phyllis left, explaining that she needed a nap, Stevie, Lisa, John, and Kate trooped in, carrying grocery bags. "Hey, Carole, you wanna help us unload?" Kate asked.

"I— Yeah, sure," said Carole.

"Great. And then we're going to make hot chocolate. We're freezing!"

Carole ran out to the pickup truck. She gathered a bundle of groceries in her arms. She looked toward the barn. She had to get out there!

"Anything wrong, Carole?" Lisa inquired, coming out to take a final load.

"What? Oh. No! Of course not," Carole replied. "I'm just taking in the scene. It's so beautiful." With that she averted her eyes and hurried into the house.

Lisa paused a moment to look, too. The Bar None was a glorious sight year-round. In winter it was starker. The ground was covered in snow and the mountains looked more forbidding. When it got dark—at five in the afternoon—and the coyotes started to howl, the vastness of the landscape was almost frightening. If a person ever stayed out there at night . . . Lisa shivered a little, thinking about it. For someone like John Brightstar, who had grown up out here, this territory was home. But Lisa knew in her heart that she would always feel more comfortable in suburban Willow Creek.

"Hurry up with that bag!" Kate called. "We've got the milk on for hot chocolate!"

"The milk?" Lisa asked, entering the kitchen a moment later. "I thought you used water for hot chocolate."

"That's the instant kind. But Christine's mom showed me how to make the real stuff, from cocoa powder, sugar, and milk," Kate replied.

"So I guess everyone has to learn cooking secrets from other people's moms, huh?" Lisa said, glad that she wasn't the only one.

"Or dads," John reminded them. "My dad makes the best pancakes this side of the Mississippi."

"Oh, good," said Lisa, "then we don't have to argue. Because *Carole's* dad makes the best on our side of the Mississippi! When we have slumber parties, he has to churn them out for hours!"

Carole made an effort to laugh with everyone else. She hoped it didn't sound too fake. All she wanted to do was leave. She just had to get away, soon, but she didn't know how to escape without answering a ton of questions. She gave a frustrated sigh. Sometimes The Saddle Club was almost too close. This was one of those times. If she said anything about the black mare, Stevie and Lisa would get those concerned looks. They didn't understand the instant bond she had formed with the mare. It wasn't that the mare resembled Cobalt, although that was what had initially drawn Carole to her. Now it was more the fact that she needed Carole, pure and simple. Stevie and Lisa thought they understood, but they didn't.

After a mug or two of cocoa, Stevie wanted everyone to play board games. The temperature had dropped five degrees from the day before; it was bitterly cold and windy, a perfect inside day.

Kate went to the basement and came up with a pile of games. "Monopoly? Risk? Parcheesi? We've got all the old standards. Cards? Uno? Carole, what do you want to play?" she asked. Carole looked a little out of it, and Kate wanted to make sure she felt included.

"Uh, I don't really care," Carole said distractedly. "But um, whatever it is, why don't you guys set it up and I'll be back in a minute."

"Where are you off to, Car'?" Stevie asked.

Carole met her friend's hazel eyes for a moment. "I've got to run back to the bunkhouse," she said evenly. She didn't explain further. Setting her mug down on the nearest table, she headed for the door.

Stevie went to the window and watched her go. She noticed that instead of heading for the bunkhouse, Carole went to the barn.

"She must be going out to see the mare," Stevie mused aloud.

"Do you think so?" Lisa said anxiously. "I wonder why she didn't tell us."

The two of them watched Carole's progress across the snow.

John spoke up tentatively. "If I were you, I'd cut her some slack," he said. "The mare needs her."

Lisa was a little annoyed. This was Saddle Club business. Why was John interfering?

"Look," said John, as if he could read her mind, "I know I'm butting in here, but I've watched her with the horse, and Carole's—she—I don't know how to put this, but she's really got a way with her."

Something in John's tone made Lisa glance up at him, despite her irritation. "What are you saying?"

"Yeah, I mean, we all know Carole's great with horses," said Stevie.

John looked uncomfortable. "I can't explain it. It's just a feeling I have. I'll know more when I've seen them together more."

Lisa's and John's eyes met. He seemed to be pleading with her to understand. Maybe he was right. Maybe she and Stevie were getting too worked up about a nonexistent problem. Clearly Carole felt hedged in by them. Maybe they ought to take a different tactic and not be so nosy. They *all* knew what it was like when The Saddle Club got so tight that there was no breathing room. Once

90

in a while each one of them needed space from the other two. That was only natural.

"Well, tell us if you come to any conclusions," she said lightly.

John looked relieved. He thanked Kate for the cocoa and excused himself. "I've been having so much fun this morning, I kind of forgot I have a job to do," he said on his way out.

"Maybe he's right," Stevie said when he had gone. "Maybe we should quit worrying about 'what if.'"

"I was thinking that, too," Lisa said. "I only wish I believed Carole was enjoying the present. This whole trip she's been somewhere else."

Eventually the three girls settled down to a game of gin rummy. Stevie was the dealer. When she started to hand out the first cards, she made three piles. She hesitated a moment, then went back to the first pile. They all knew there was no point in dealing a hand for Carole.

IT WAS CAROLE'S worst nightmare. The black mare was trotting along the corral fence, back and forth, back and forth. She was covered in sweat. Judging from the deep, muddy tracks, she'd been at it all morning. Every so often, she stopped and whinnied. The sound pierced Carole to the core. She ran blindly toward the fence. The mare was so agitated, she didn't notice Carole at first. But when Carole slipped throught the fence, whispering to her, the mare listened immediately. She came up to Carole of her own accord. Carole felt herself smile inside. It was the first time the mare had come to her and not vice versa.

"Let's get you out of here," Carole said. She opened the gate and led the mare through. It didn't even occur to her that she had no lead line or bridle or any kind of equipment for controlling the mare. Her one thought was to help the mare.

The mare followed, docile as a school horse. On the other side of the gate, she seemed to calm down even more. Soon she was rubbing her head against Carole. Carole glanced around. She wanted to take the mare away from the barn, even for a little while. But walking would take forever. Without stopping to think of the possible consequences, Carole climbed up on the fence. She placed her hands on the mare's withers. In another second she had sprung up onto the jet-black back. The mare seemed slightly surprised to have her aboard, but she didn't seem to mind. Carole laughed when the horse turned around to look at her rider, an inquisitive expression in her large eyes. "That's right. We're taking a little bareback excursion," Carole said. In response, the mare opened her mouth and nibbled on the toe of Carole's shoe.

Carole used her knees and seat to guide the mare toward the trailhead. It was as easy as if she'd had a bridle and saddle. The mare seemed to know where Carole wanted to go. She jogged along at a steady pace. As soon as they were a few hundred yards down the trail, Carole got off again. The mare nuzzled her.

"Come on, girl," Carole murmured. She wanted to see if the mare would follow her. Sure enough, when she walked, the mare walked behind her. When she stopped, the mare stopped. It was almost like playing with a dog! Carole spent the better part of an hour playing tag. It made her heart fill with joy to see the mare relaxed and playful.

"Okay, you stand still now. Pretend you're on the cross-ties," Carole said. She gave the mare's neck and back a massage, using techniques she had read about in her favorite magazine, *Horse and Horseman*. The massaging really seemed to work. By the time she was through, the mare was so loose she looked as if she might fall asleep. One hind hoof was cocked and her head was low, her lower lip hanging. "If only we could stay here," Carole said aloud. In the woods she could sense her connection with the mare more powerfully than at the barn. She couldn't explain it, but she understood the mare and felt the mare trusted her. It was quiet and peaceful away from the ranch.

But all too soon it was time to go back. If they stayed away too long, their absence would be noticed. Trying to swallow the lump in her throat, Carole found a log and swung herself aboard. She rode back at a snail's pace, letting the mare meander back up the trail.

When she came into view of the ranch, Carole tried

giving the mare a few cues to see how she would respond. She asked her to halt, jog, halt, walk, and turn. Every time, the mare obeyed. But it was strange. Carole knew she was obeying because she wanted to, not because she had to. She was *letting* Carole direct her. Carole leaned down to pat the mare's neck. When she sat back up, her heart skipped a beat. There, standing in front of the barn, were Frank and his crew of wranglers. They were all staring at Carole.

"Amazing!" somebody called.

Somebody else started clapping.

Carole was dismayed that everyone had seen. She had only meant to help the mare. Now she was yet again the center of attention. Nervously she continued forward. She coaxed the mare toward the group of people. What could she say to Frank now? Would he be angry that she had ridden off without telling him? Without saddling up first? Without trying the mare in an enclosed area?

"I—I'm sorry. I know it was stupid, but—"

The expression on Frank's face was one of respect, not disapproval. "I wouldn't have believed it if I hadn't seen it myself. How on earth did you get her to settle down enough to get on?"

"Yeah, and how'd you get her to go in the direction you wanted?" Mick asked. "And to stop like that?"

Carole was embarrassed by the attention. She couldn't think of a thing to say. She searched the crowd of stable hands until she saw John Brightstar. He was looking at her steadily, wisely. He understood! She wasn't sure she understood, herself, whatever it was that made the mare trust her. But if John understood, it seemed okay.

The wranglers pressed Carole for an explanation, so she gave a response that was becoming almost automatic. "I don't know," she said.

THERE WAS A PAUSE. Then so much happened all at once that Carole couldn't get a word in edgewise. Frank turned to go inside and tend to business. Everybody else wanted to see the black mare that had run away the day before, that Carole had ridden bareback without a bridle. One of the stable hands came up with a lead line and halter. Another helped Carole to the ground. Nobody seemed to notice that the mare was beginning to toss her head nervously. It was as if they thought that because she trusted Carole, she now trusted all humans. Carole knew she had better explain—and fast.

"We'll groom her for you," Mick volunteered.

"Yeah, she'll look great when she's all shined up," said someone else.

Only John objected. "Maybe we should let Carole—"

But before he could finish, and before Carole could open her mouth to protest, the mare had been led off to be cross-tied. Carole ran behind, struggling to cut through the group. It was too late! The mare panicked. The minute the cross-ties were snapped to her halter, she started backing up. She backed up so hard that the snaps quick-released from the wall. Lines flapping, the mare bolted wildly down the aisle.

"Somebody get her!"

Carole stood there paralyzed. *Run*, she prayed silently. *Run as fast as you can.*

This time the wranglers were on their toes. One put up his hands to stop her. She ducked left—right toward Mick. Mick put up his hand lightning fast. He caught her.

Carole flinched when she heard the command: "Better put her in a stall till she quiets down."

Helplessly Carole watched as the mare was led away down the aisle, dancing nervously at the end of the lead shank. As she turned the corner of the aisle, she let out a loud, plaintive whinny. Carole blocked her ears with her hands. She couldn't bear the sound. If only there were something, anything, she could do!

PHYLLIS WAS LAUGHING so hard, tears were running down her cheeks. "Mom, what *is* it?" Kate demanded testily.

97

Stevie and Lisa had an inkling of what was so funny. Phyllis had just examined the groceries they'd bought. Then she had asked them to explain their purchases. Stevie and Lisa were attempting this when Kate walked in. "Allspice! You thought I meant 'all spices.' That's great! It's a classic!"

"Oh," Kate said, a grin breaking over her features. "Oh, that is funny."

Stevie and Lisa waited. And they waited. Eventually the Devines would have to stop laughing and explain.

Finally Phyllis managed to breathe in and out. "There's a spice *called* allspice," she said. "It's like cinnamon or nutmeg, only its name is allspice."

"Oh," said Stevie.

"I see," said Lisa.

"Now, where's that pastry flour?" Kate's mother inquired.

Lisa gulped "Um, we got some pastry and some flour. What's pastry flour?"

Phyllis smothered her laughter. "I think we'd better start at the beginning," she said.

A half hour later the girls had sorted through the list. Their faces were bright crimson. Crushed tomatoes were canned tomatoes crushed for making sauces. Condensed milk was a sweetened, canned milk product used for baking. And *chicken* meant a whole chicken, plain and simple.

"I have to admit, that did cross my mind," Stevie said about the last mistake.

"Are you going to have the right ingredients for dinner?" Lisa asked. Even though Phyllis didn't seem to care, she felt like a total idiot.

"Yes," Phyllis said. "Because I've decided that dinner is going to be leftovers. I don't feel the greatest, and I don't feel like making a big meal, anyway."

Stevie, Lisa, and Kate were concerned, but Phyllis brushed them off. "No, no, please—it's only a cold. But I thought you guys could heat up the leftovers and I could go to bed early."

Lisa looked at Stevie. Stevie looked at Lisa. This time they both had a mischievous glint in their eyes. Stevie raised her eyebrows. Lisa nodded imperceptibly. "*We'll* make dinner!" they practically shouted.

"It's the least we can do," Stevie said.

"And we'll have fun doing it," Lisa added.

To their surprise, Phyllis looked doubtful. "Are you sure you're up to it? I mean, baking a few pies is one thing, but a full dinner for the four guests, plus six of us—you'll have to plan on dinner for ten, more if you invite Walter and John."

"No problem," Stevie assured her. After the success of the pies, she felt more confident than ever. "I've cooked for my three brothers before, and the way they eat, it's pretty much the same as cooking for ten. I'm sure we can handle it."

Lisa felt the same way. She always liked to challenge herself. This could be her next project. They could see Phyllis was wavering.

"Please!" Lisa begged. "This will be just the thing I need to ace home ec. If I can do this, I can do anything."

"I'll help them, Mom!" Kate added.

Phyllis blew her nose. She coughed slightly. She turned to Stevie and Lisa. They couldn't tell what she was thinking. They tried to look as eager as possible.

"We-ell, maybe if you made spaghetti with jar sauce and a big salad—"

"Spaghetti it is!" Stevie said. She feigned a bad Italian accent. "Lovely spaghetti with-a sauce-a from-a the jar-o. *Bon appétit!*"

"Uh, Stevie?" Lisa said.

"Yeah?"

"*Bon appétit* is French."

"Oh. Okay. *Bueno appetito?*"

Lisa smiled. "I don't think so."

"But you will let us make dinner, won't you?" Stevie pleaded.

Phyllis laughed. "All right. I can't say no to this much enthusiasm. But keep it simple!"

WHEN CAROLE RETURNED from the barn, two of her friends were hard at work. Kate had volunteered to make the salad. She was busy tearing lettuce into a wooden salad bowl. Lisa had filled a large pot with water and was hunting for smaller pots for the sauce. Stevie was looking through a stack of cookbooks. She had nothing to do right then. Her job was cooking the spaghetti, and she had already read the directions on the back of the spaghetti box—three times.

Feeling self-conscious, Carole cleared her throat. "Can I help?" she asked. No matter how upset she was about the black mare, she was not going to show it. She was going to pretend that everything was normal. She'd figure something out soon enough, and she didn't need a lot of suspicious questions from Lisa and Stevie in the meantime.

"Yeah," Lisa said, looking up in surprise. "That would be great." She told Carole the menu so far, explaining that Phyllis had gone to bed early. She consciously avoided asking about the mare. John's words had stung at first, but now that they had sunk in, she thought he might be right. If Carole wanted their help, she could ask for it. "We're wondering what else we should have with dinner."

Carole thought for a minute, glad for the distraction. "Hmmm . . . How about garlic bread? Dad and I always make that. It's really simple."

"Excellent!" Stevie exclaimed. "The more carbohydrates, the better!"

Lisa laughed. A litte enviously, she watched Carole get bread from the pantry, butter from the fridge, and garlic from the garlic braid hanging above the stove. There was something about Carole's attitude that showed confidence in the kitchen. Feeling lame, Lisa banged a jar of tomato

101

sauce on the edge of the counter to loosen the lid. She opened the jar and dumped the contents into a pot. Then she stood there stirring it. She hated to admit it, but the competitive side in her was coming out. She wanted to get credit for the dinner, too! Opening a couple of jars of sauce just didn't cut it.

Stevie dumped the spaghetti into the boiling water and re-covered the pot. Then she went back to her perch on the counter. She flipped a page in the cookbook she was studying: *Desserts from Paris, with Love!*

"*Tarte Tatin,*" she read. "Hey, this looks good! It's kind of like a fancy apple pie that's upside down. Or something. Ooh, wait: *crème brûlée.* I had this once in a restaurant with my parents. It's so good. It's pudding with burned stuff on top."

"Sounds disgusting," said Kate. "And anyway, that cookbook is ancient. Why don't you use something more up to date?"

Stevie shot her an annoyed look.

"Well, I'm all done," Kate announced. She wiped her hands briskly on her jeans and put the salad in the refrigerator.

"Me too," said Carole. She set the two long halves of French bread on a cookie tray. "These have butter and garlic on them. They just have to bake."

Lisa made a face behind her back. Why was everyone Miss Perfect Cook all of a sudden?

"Let's you and I go set the table," Kate suggested. "Boy, this sure is fun, cooking together, isn't it?"

"Yeah," said Lisa, barely able to hide her sarcasm. When they were gone, she ran over to Stevie. "Are you thinking what I'm thinking?"

"They're going to get all the credit!" Stevie answered. Her competitive blood was up, too.

"Exactly!" said Lisa.

Stevie's eyes narrowed. "But not if we knock their socks off with a fabulous French dessert! Let's make *crème brûlée* and *tarte Tatin*!"

It was too good a suggestion to ignore. The two girls whizzed into action. Stevie got out eggs, milk, butter, and flour. Lisa found apples and began to peel them. They worked at a feverish pace, running back and forth to consult the recipes.

"Ow!" Lisa screamed. "I cut my thumb!"

"Are you okay?" Stevie asked, ambulances and hospitals flashing through her mind.

"Forget *me*!" Lisa cried. "There's blood on the apples!"

Stevie ran over to look. "Gross!"

"It's not my fault!" Lisa snapped.

"I know, I know! But you're going to have to throw them out."

Lisa could have screamed. She looked into the bloodied bowl of apples. All that work for nothing! It was enough to—

There was a loud clattering sound. Both girls turned and looked at the stove. "The spaghetti!" Stevie shrieked. The pot was boiling over. Water was spilling onto the stove at an alarming rate.

"What the— You put the top back on!" Lisa screeched. "Even I know you're not supposed to do that!"

"I forgot!" Stevie wailed.

"Turn off the burner!" Lisa cried, reaching for the oven mitts.

Stevie lunged for the closest knob and turned it all the way. Unfortunately, it was the wrong burner. More unfortunately, she turned the heat up, not off. And even more unfortunately, the oven mitts happened to be resting on that very burner—and Lisa happened to be grabbing for them.

"Aaaaaaaaaahhhhhhhhhh!" Lisa's bloodcurdling roar resounded through the house. In the dining room Kate and Carole dropped the basket of flatware. Next door Frank shot out of his office. Upstairs Phyllis tore out of her bedroom. They all came running into the kitchen as fast as they could.

"What on earth—"

"Stop! Drop! And roll!" Stevie shouted.

Lisa took a huge pot of water and threw it at the stove, where a small fire had erupted. She missed. She soaked the Devines.

At that moment Stevie managed to get the kitchen fire extinguisher to work. She drenched the stove. She also drenched the pantry, the table, the cupboards, and the floor to be safe. For a second the kitchen was dead quiet. Stevie cleared her throat. "I'm afraid dinner is going to be a little late," she announced.

THAT EVENING, BACK in the bunkhouse, the girls giggled into the night. They all agreed that the McHughs and the Martins had to be the best guests ever—second only to The Saddle Club.

"At least, The Saddle Club when we're not cooking," Stevie joked. After the kitchen fiasco, the two couples had volunteered to drive into town and pick up pizza for everyone. That, Carole's garlic bread, and the salad had made a great meal.

"The only problem now is how we're ever going to live this down!" Lisa wailed. "I'm beginning to think I deserve an F in home ec, not a B-minus. I've burned toast before, but I've never come so close to burning a house down!"

From their beds Stevie and Carole laughed. It was good to hear Lisa making jokes about her grades. They knew that when the time came, she would work like crazy to get an A, the way she always did. But a few months ago she wouldn't even have been able to make jokes about it.

"Oh, well, we'll figure it out in the morning," said Stevie. She was suddenly hit by a wave of tiredness. Kitchen trauma was exhausting!

"Good idea," said Lisa. "I'm bushed."

"Night," said Carole.

Slowly the girls drifted off to sleep—at least Stevie and Lisa did. Carole lay in bed, tensely poised. She was waiting for the time when she could escape to the barn. When the others were breathing steadily, she got up. With methodic movements, she pulled her boots on. Ever so quietly, she opened the door of the bunkhouse. Lisa stirred and opened one eye—just in time to see her friend disappearing into the night.

As soon as she was outside, Carole felt a wave of relief mixed with apprehension. She could finally have an uninterrupted visit with the black mare. But how would that help the horse in the long run? It seemed as if everyone were conspiring against her—against them both. The cold and her eagerness to get there made Carole sprint to the barn. She walked directly to the mare's stall, opened the door, and slipped inside. The mare came toward her out of the shadows. Whispering to her, Carole led the horse noiselessly through the barn and out into the night. She hopped up on her back. The mare began to walk toward the trail, then to jog. It broke Carole's heart to have to stop her, to will her to turn around and go back. If only Frank would see things differently! If only he could forget about his investment and do what was right for the mare! "I know how you feel," she said aloud. "I honestly do." She reached down and patted the black shoulder. "I feel like I belong with those horses, too." The plan that had been forming deep in her consciousness pricked at her

106

mind. Slowly it came to her that she knew what she was going to do—what she had to do.

But still, for a long time Carole sat on the mare's tall back in the moonlight. She was filled with fear—or not exactly fear: Somehow she knew she would be safe with the mare. It was more a combination of guilt and misgivings that wouldn't go away. She could almost hear the voice of her riding instructor, Max, echoing in her head: "Never ride alone without telling someone where you're going." What would Max say to her riding alone, intending, planning, hoping to keep her destination a secret? To her taking a horse that wasn't rightfully hers? To her riding without tack on territory she didn't know well at all? Shutting her mind to hundreds of doubts, Carole nudged the mare forward. She was doing the right thing. She had promised the black mare that she would help her, and she wasn't going to break her word.

WALKING HOME, JOHN Brightstar almost didn't see the horse and rider in the near distance. The horse was black and the rider was wearing dark clothing, so they blended into the darkness. But once he noticed them, there was no doubt in his mind who it was. He stopped and listened. Just as he expected, he could hear faint whispers floating toward him. He cocked his head. He hesitated. Then he continued on his way home.

CAROLE WASN'T THERE when Stevie and Lisa woke up. Lisa took one look at the empty bunk and was sure her friend had slept in the mare's stall.

Stevie seemed to have the same idea. The fact that she didn't say anything proved it. Neither of them mentioned Carole's absence. All of a sudden it had become a forbidden topic. It seemed as if whoever pointed it out first would be the bad friend—the overprotective, interfering friend.

"Ready for breakfast?" Lisa asked briskly. She was determined not to tell Stevie about having seen Carole go out the night before.

"Sure! Whenever you are!" Stevie replied, her voice a little too eager.

Soon they were too preoccupied to worry, though. At breakfast, despite the fact that neither of the girls ate much cereal or toast, they filled up pretty quickly—on humble pie.

Kate set the tone. She sat down at the table and looked across at her father. "Dad, did you forget to take a shower this morning?" she asked innocently. "Oh, right," she said, grinning wickedly at the two members of The Saddle Club, "I forgot: You had one last night, courtesy of Lisa!"

Frank chuckled.

Stevie glared. She tried to change the subject. "Gosh, another cold day," she said pointedly.

Frank looked at her sternly. "Look, if you're cold, just tell me, Stevie. Honestly. I don't want you to feel you have to use the whole house for kindling!"

The Martins and McHughs tittered. "Don't worry," one of the wives said, "you'll soon be marvelous cooks. You've already perfected a very difficult technique: the flambé!"

"Flambé?" Lisa asked, knowing she was setting herself up.

"Right. That's when the chef lights a dish on fire. Of course, he usually restrains himself to the one dish . . ."

"You know, I think I understand why they changed the name from home economics to nutrition and household management," said Kate.

"You do?" Lisa asked in a small voice.

"Sure! It's not all that *economical* to burn down the family ranch!"

In the midst of the laughter that followed, John Brightstar appeared at the door. He often turned up at breakfast to grab a bite and get instructions from Frank. He took one look at Lisa and began to grin. "Heard you had a *hot time* last night," he said.

Everyone guffawed except Lisa and Stevie. Lisa scowled. Stevie gave the entire table her haughtiest look. She stood up. She summoned what shreds of dignity she still had. "Has *Mrs.* Devine eaten breakfast yet?"

Kate shook her head. Stevie pulled Lisa up by the elbow. "Do excuse us. We need to see to the comfort of the lady of the house."

"Uh, yeah," Lisa said. Bright crimson, the two of them fled the scene.

They got tea and toast from the kitchen, put it on a tray, and marched upstairs to Phyllis and Frank's bedroom. The only good thing about all the teasing was that it had made them allies again, and both girls knew it.

"We'll never live it down!" Lisa wailed.

Phyllis sat up in bed and laughed. "You already have with me," she said. She eyed the breakfast appreciatively. "I ought to get the flu more often. Now tell me the whole story, start to finish."

Stevie and Lisa flopped down in chairs. "Lisa and I thought it would be fun to make a fancy dessert."

"Like *tarte* . . ."

"*Tatin*," Stevie supplied.

"Yeah, or *crème* . . ."

"*Brûlée*," finished Stevie.

"So we found a couple of recipes, and—"

Phyllis opened her eyes wide. She was staring at them with dismay. "You didn't use that French dessert cookbook, did you?" The girls nodded. "No! That cookbook is a curse! It ruined my first dinner party ever. I should have thrown it out then!"

Now Lisa and Stevie were all ears. "Your first dinner party ever was ruined?" Lisa asked, taken aback. She couldn't imagine Kate's efficient, creative mother having a kitchen fiasco of her own.

"Yes, it was terrible!" said Phyllis. "It was when Frank and I were first married. He was in the Corps, and he'd invited his superior over for dinner, and the man's wife. Little did the woman know that when she said yes to the invitation, she was also saying yes to getting tomato soup spilled on her best dress, having her hair scorched . . ."

Beaming, Stevie and Lisa settled in for a long story. This was the kind of home economics they could take!

CAROLE FELT STRANGE. In a way, she had never been so afraid in her whole life. But in another way, she had never been so calm. She had a purpose, a mission: to set the black mare free. "And you won't ever have to come back," she promised. The mare seemed to nod as if she understood.

After hatching her plan, Carole had returned to the stable and slept in the mare's stall. She had ridden away at dawn, before anyone could stop her. The sun was rising in the sky now, but the frigid February wind cut through her jacket. The thought of what she was wearing made her smile. She had been too afraid of getting caught to go back to the bunkhouse, so she was still clad in her long under-wear, flannel pajamas, and boots. And the mare looked like a backyard pony, being ridden with nothing but a halter and lead shank.

Another thought made Carole stop smiling, though. It made her feel sad and lonely: the fact that Stevie's and Lisa's waking up would have meant getting caught. At one time Carole would have told her friends everything. They would have helped her plan the escape. Heck, they would have insisted on coming with her. But the black mare had come between them. And right now, something inside Carole was telling her that she had to put the horse first.

"We're almost there, girl," Carole whispered. They were. They had reached the frozen creek and were nearing the mountain. As soon as she found the herd, Carole was going to set the mare free. After that she was going to try to scare the herd off so that they wouldn't come back for a while. When Frank saw how happy the mare was in the wild . . . Well, Carole hadn't thought much beyond that. But she was certain a dramatic gesture like this would change his mind. Shivering, she pulled her coat tighter.

Minutes later the mare raised her head and sniffed the air. Carole tensed, listening for the stallion. They had walked on a little farther when she heard the whinny. The mare heard it, too. She neighed back at the top of her lungs. Her body shook so hard that Carole laughed. Carole nudged the mare forward. She didn't want to let her go until she had joined the herd. "Come on, girl, let's walk on up," she urged. But the mare had other plans. She gathered her body underneath her and sprang forward! Carole nearly had the breath knocked out of her. She clung to the black mare as the mare raced toward the stallion's whinny.

The pace was blinding. The ground sped by in a blur of white. Carole felt tears in her eyes. It was the fastest she had ever ridden in her life. They galloped over the snow toward the mountain. All at once there was another horse galloping beside them. It was the stallion himself! He raced the mare until, his teeth bared, he began to turn her toward the herd. Carole was certain she would fall off. Her arms and legs ached. She couldn't hold on any longer. She felt herself slipping, slipping . . . She closed her eyes.

The mare slowed and stopped. Carole opened her eyes. She sat up. They had come to a secluded knoll at the base of the mountain. It looked out over the creek. There was snow above them and below them. The stallion had led them there. He had led them to his home and his herd. Carole counted seven mares, three of which were heavy with foals. Two had foals by their sides already. Blinking into the sunlight, Carole had to rub her eyes. She felt as if she'd died and gone to heaven.

She still had a task to do, though. Gently she took off the mare's halter, winding the lead shank around it. To her surprise, the mare didn't run away. She stood by Carole. She seemed to be waiting for some cue. "I don't know what to say, girl," Carole said. "Mission accomplished, I guess." The mare tossed her head up and down. Still she didn't move from Carole's side.

There was one thing Carole wanted to do before she shooed the horses away and started on the long, long walk back. She wanted to talk to the stallion. Slowly she went toward him with her hand out. With every step she waited for him to dash off, but he stood his ground. Carole whispered to him and he almost seemed to whisper back. His nostrils fluttered. She touched his silky nose. He butted his head against her. The black mare joined them. Pretty soon the other mares began to amble over, curious, their ears pricked. Carole laughed aloud. They were accepting her! Even though she was a part of the human world, they trusted her. Carole went around to each of the horses, stroking them and talking to them. She played with the foals. She praised the mares for being good mothers. In the midst of getting to know the herd, something dawned on her: This was the only chance she would have in her life to be like this with wild horses. Soon she would be back with people, back in school, back having to explain all the time. "I guess I wanted to be set free, too," she murmured to the nearest horse, a hardy-looking pinto. In response, he snorted loudly. Carole laughed. "I agree!" she said.

All too soon the afternoon sun began to wane. Carole had forgotten that it got dark so early. She turned to the black mare. It was time to say good-bye. A lump had formed in her throat and stuck there.

Carole knew she had done the right thing, but it didn't make leaving any easier. And she was very, very tired. She had barely slept at all in the mare's stall. She'd been too busy plotting their escape. It suddenly occurred to her that she hadn't eaten anything all day except a candy bar that she had found in her pocket. She was hungry and thirsty. Her throat felt a little scratchy, too. She was probably coming down with the flu Phyllis had.

It was also hard to leave knowing she had to walk about five hours through the snow. She reached down to grab a handful of snow. At least that would wet her whistle. As she bent down, Carole lost her balance. "Whoops!" She sat hard in the snow. She made a halfhearted move to get up, but it was actually very comfortable sitting on the ground. The snow was soft and warm. The black mare came over and nudged her gently.

Carole smiled. She put her head back for a moment. Then she put it all the way back. She lay down in the snow. It was pure bliss. "I'll just sleep for ten minutes," she said aloud. She closed her eyes. Dimly she sensed the mare nudging her . . . and nudging her again . . .

CAROLE WAS HAVING the strangest dreams. First she dreamed she was riding the black mare. It was nighttime. The stars were very bright. She was more tired than she had ever been in her life. Then she dreamed that all her friends were coming in to see her. First Stevie and Lisa came, then Christine and Kate. Frank and Phyllis came, then John and Walter. And all around her was the herd of wild horses. Carole could talk to them, just like before. She knew what they were thinking, and they understood her. Sighing in her sleep, Carole rolled over.

But then her dream became a nightmare. Someone was taking the black mare from her. They put her in a stall and clanged the door shut. They bolted it with five bolts.

Carole had to help her! She had to help her escape again! "Let her go!" Carole cried. She sat up with a start. Her heart was racing. She was utterly disoriented. Then she made out a trophy by the bed. The name on it was Kate Devine. So she was in Kate's room? "Why am I in here?" Carole said aloud.

A familiar voice answered, "Kate gave up her room for you till you get better. She's staying in the bunkhouse with us."

"Oh, I see." Carole leaned back on the pillows and closed her eyes.

"Darn, I thought she was waking up," the voice said.

Carole's eyes flew open again. Lisa was sitting on a chair beside the bed. John was with her. "Lisa? John? Wait, *what*? Till I get better? Am I sick?"

"Yay! You are awake!" Lisa exclaimed. "We were so worried about you, Carole, but you're going to be fine. Your fever's nearly gone, and—"

"And you'll be back in the saddle in no time," John supplied.

Startled, Carole looked from Lisa to John. She *was* sick! Other than that, she knew nothing. She had no idea what time it was, what day it was. The last thing she remembered was saying good-bye to the black mare!

"The mare. What happened to her?" she whispered urgently.

Lisa smiled, nudging John. "I knew that would be the first thing you asked. And don't worry, she's fine, too."

"Absolutely fine," John echoed.

At that moment there was a knock on the door and Frank entered the room. "I thought I heard voices in here."

"Excellent timing, boss," said John. "Carole just woke up, and she asked about the mare."

Frank smiled broadly. "Then I guess you've heard that she's fine and she misses you."

"She misses me?" Carole repeated dumbly. How would Frank know that? The black mare should have been far away by now.

"Yes. Mick and the boys told me to tell you that she wants you to get better and get outside to see her just as soon as you can."

Carole felt her stomach turn over. "Outside? But—"

"You know she saved your life, don't you, Carole?" Lisa asked quietly, with a quick glance at her friend. "You would have frozen to death. Instead you came away with frostbite and strep throat."

At Carole's perplexed look, Frank said, "Maybe we'd better start from the beginning. John, why don't you give it a go?"

"Sure, boss." John cleared his throat and began.

Carole listened, mesmerized, as she heard her own story.

"We wouldn't have known where you were if the black mare hadn't come home and found us," John began

118

gravely. "I've heard of dogs leading people to their masters, but horses? Never. But that's exactly what she did. Kate saw her wander in loose close to dinnertime. That's when I knew something was wrong. The Devines organized a search party and we set out. I brought the mare with me, ponying her off Tex. I figured you'd be up by the mountain, where we went before. We got there and couldn't see a thing." John paused for a breath. Carole shifted nervously under her layers of blankets. She desperately wanted John to skip to the end of the story. She wanted to know the worst!

"All of a sudden, the mare started whinnying. The stallion whinnied back, and they kept it up, back and forth, till finally we found them two hundred yards up on the overlook."

"Darnedest thing I ever saw," Frank put in, shaking his head in wonder.

"The stallion had the herd gathered off in the distance," John continued. "He was standing over you himself. At first I didn't know why he was there. Then I got close enough that I could make out your coat. The stallion ran off a little ways, but he waited until Frank and the others and I were by your side. When we picked you up and put you on the mare, he rounded up the herd." John's voice sank to a murmur. "I—I guess he knew his job was done," he said.

"And the mare?" Carole asked.

119

"She's . . . here," John said.

"She's back at home, just as safe as can be. You can ride her again, the minute you're well," Frank added encouragingly. "Only this time, *tell* us if you're going off on a long trail ride. Please!"

Carole felt the color drain from her face. She sat back against the pillows. Then she had failed! Frank didn't even understand why she had ridden off! He thought she had taken a trail ride! A pleasure ride! The mare had lost her chance to go free.

Carole was so distracted, she barely heard Frank's next words. "I think you'll find the mare a changed horse," he said. "Would you agree, John?"

John nodded but looked at Carole. "Yes, I would," he said slowly. "And I mean that."

"This past day and a half she's been a lot quieter around the barn. It's funny," Frank mused. "She seems to have chosen *us* finally."

Carole frowned. Maybe Frank had misinterpreted the mare's behavior. But that would be odd—Frank was an excellent horseman. And it would be stranger still for John *and* Frank to be off. "What do you mean?" she asked.

Frank's forehead wrinkled in concentration. "Well, it's like I've seen with a lot of horses that come off the range. At a certain point, they realize that life 'on the inside' isn't too bad."

"Usually there's a person who helps them come to that understanding," John added. Carole had the feeling he was saying what he said for Frank's benefit as much as for hers. "With the mare, it was you."

"That's right," Frank said. "When you were out riding and fell off, she might have run off with the herd. But she didn't. She came back to us—to get help for you. Anyway, the experience seems to have mellowed her somewhat."

Frank gave Carole's shoulder a squeeze. "Hurry and get well," he said.

Carole's head was reeling. Could what Frank said be true? Could the mare have chose civilization of her own accord? Now Carole really couldn't concentrate. She barely heard Lisa tell her to get some rest. She was asleep by the time Lisa said, "We'll stay right here in case you need anything."

STEVIE AND LISA were chopping, slicing, and dicing excitedly. Over the past two days, Phyllis had helped them choose a menu for their big dinner. She had helped them shop for it. She had given them a game plan. Now they were carrying out the plan.

"This dinner is more than your home ec dinner," Stevie said, slicing a mushroom. "It's Carole's get-well dinner *and* our last-night-at-the-ranch dinner."

"And don't forget, it's also our attempt-to-redeem-ourselves dinner," Lisa added.

Both of them knew without saying it that Carole's getting better was the most important. All reports had been good. Carole had been awake and talking for most of the day. She had even wandered into the kitchen to taste-test the soup stock.

John Brightstar popped his head into the kitchen. "Need any help? I'm all done outside."

"Yeah, you can chop carrots," Stevie said, handing him a bunch.

"I heard Carole's been up," said John.

"Yup, she's doing a lot better," Lisa answered. "How's her favorite horse?"

"Good. She's still a little standoffish with us, but she's acting a lot happier. She ate all her dinner for the first time last night."

"That's great!" said Lisa, thrilled that they would have good news for Carole.

"You know," John added tentatively, "the boss thinks Carole was out riding and fell off."

There was a long, pregnant pause. The girls had worried that John would bring this up.

"And?" Lisa said finally.

John looked down. He shifted uncomfortably. "And I don't think that's exactly what happened."

Stevie and Lisa exchanged glances. "We *know* it's not," Stevie said. The night before, Lisa had filled her in on what she'd seen and what Frank had said to Carole in Kate's room. Both of them felt terrible. By worrying too much that there was *going* to be a problem, they had created a problem. Carole hadn't felt comfortable sharing

122

her plan with her closest friends. If she had, they could have tried to talk her out of it or, more likely, gone with her and made sure she was okay.

Lisa put down her paring knife. "Are you going to tell Frank the truth?"

"No," John said without hesitation. "No way. What he doesn't know—"

"—can't hurt Carole," Stevie finished. "That's what we decided. And Frank might take it the wrong way if he found out The Saddle Club was trying to reduce his stock for him by letting one of his horses go free."

John let out a sigh. "Phew. For a minute there I was afraid maybe I was breaking news. But you guys were right. There *was* something to worry about with Carole's attachment to the black mare."

"No, you were right," said Stevie generously. "We should have been more understanding and less suspicious of Carole. Then she would have at least had allies. She wouldn't have had to go off alone." Stevie was not prone to displays of emotion. She prided herself on being cool and tough. But she felt herself choking up slightly at the idea of Carole's worrying about the black mare all alone. "Boy, these onions will get you every time!" she said briskly. She grabbed one and hastily began to peel it.

Lisa looked over at John. A little shyly she asked, "Did you ever figure out what it was about Carole that you couldn't figure out before?"

John nodded seriously. He was silent for a moment. Then he said slowly, "I think I did. I think the reason Carole was more upset about the black mare's suffering was that she . . . she actually sensed it more than the rest of us."

Stevie and Lisa were utterly still, listening. They had suspected something like this for months—years. But nobody had ever put it into words.

"Carole has a gift with horses, a very unusual gift. I'm not sure even she understands it. The only reason I picked up on it is that some of my ancestors were supposed to have had the same gift." John paused with the carrots. "I think Carole is what they call a horse whisperer."

The girls let the phrase sink in. It was the perfect way of describing how Carole communicated with horses.

"What exactly is a horse whisperer?" Lisa asked, even though she thought she knew.

"Well," said John slowly, "a horse whisperer is someone who communicates with a horse almost as if she were another horse; as if she and the horse share the same language. It's a kind of natural horsemanship, teaching a horse without breaking its spirit and letting the horse decide when to join you. I can't really explain it, but once you've seen it, you never forget it. Have you ever seen Carole display unusual abilities with animals, like being able to approach wild horses and 'talk' to them?"

Stevie grinned. "There aren't too many mustangs in Willow Creek," she joked, breaking the spell. But she and

Lisa both knew what John meant. Carole communicated with horses on a different level than normal people. The black mare was a perfect example of that. She had been wild, and Carole had tamed her. She had "spoken" to her, and somehow the mare had known she would be all right, at least when Carole was nearby.

"Say, did we ever find out the black mare's name?" Lisa asked suddenly.

Stevie shook her head. "Nope. Kate asked her dad and he said he didn't know, either."

"I tried thinking of some," John volunteered, "but none of them seemed to suit her."

"Hmmm," Lisa said, her eyes far away. "Interesting . . ."

CAROLE WALKED INTO the barn a little shakily. She felt okay, really, just a little tired. She was more worried about how she would react to seeing the mare.

Mick and John met her at the door. John gave Carole a big hug. Mick went to shake her hand. Then he said, "Aw, heck, I'll hug you, too," and enveloped her in a bear hug. "Bet I know who you came to see," the wrangler guessed. "I've got some carrots for her right here." He patted his jacket pocket.

"Great," Carole said. She didn't have the heart to tell him that the mare probably wouldn't take the treats.

Carole let herself be led down the aisle. She expected Mick to stop at the mare's stall. Instead he continued on to the grooming area. The mare was standing there cross-tied!

Carole did a double take. The horse that a few days earlier wouldn't put up with the ties seemed to have gotten used to them overnight. She pushed her nose out toward Carole. Incredulous, Carole rubbed the black forehead.

"Now, that's one thing she won't let us do," Mick commented. "She won't let us go near her face. I hope it's only a matter of time, but I don't know."

On further examination, the mare was a little jittery, a little high-strung. But lots of horses were that way. Obviously she wasn't going to metamorphose into a dull school horse—and anyway, nobody wanted her to.

Mick put his hand out toward the mare. She raised her head suspiciously and backed up a step. "See? Oh, well, what can you do?"

"Here, wait," said Carole. "Where are those carrots?"

Mick handed her a bunch.

Carole fed two to the mare. "Come here," she said to Mick.

"By you?"

"Yes."

Carole slipped the stable hand a carrot. "Okay, feed it to her."

Mick put out his hand. The mare laid her ears back. "Aw, forget it, I—"

"No, wait!" said Carole. She was aware of John watching her. She rubbed the mare's neck soothingly and said to her, "You know Mick. He's your friend, the way we all are here. So you can act nice to everyone, okay?" Carole went on murmuring, her voice barely a whisper. Eventually the mare blew through her nostrils.

Bingo! Carole thought. "Try again," she said to Mick.

Mick sidled up close to the mare and again proffered the carrot. After a moment's hesitation, the mare put her head down and plucked it from his hand. Mick grinned from ear to ear. "She took it!" he exclaimed. Carole urged John over, then another wrangler who was watching the scene. Slowly, one by one, and with the help of carrots, each of them made friends with the black mare.

When the carrots were gone, the mare looked around. Carole was scratching her withers. John was standing at her head. The mare turned and rubbed her forehead against John.

"Well, how do you like that?" John murmured.

"It's . . . It's great," Carole said. She felt her throat getting tight. This was the sign she had been waiting for, ever since Frank had told her of the mare's change. It meant, simply, that the mare wasn't going to be a one-woman horse forever. It was Carole's dream come true that the mare was starting to like it, as Frank had said, "on the inside." But it didn't change the fact that Carole was going home tomorrow, and that she was losing the mare to the Bar None.

* * *

THEIR ELEVEN GUESTS were assembled around the table. The cheese-and-cracker hors d'oeuvres had been eaten. Dessert was in the oven. And to Stevie and Lisa, the most beautiful words on earth were the ones Phyllis proclaimed on their behalf: "Dinner is served!"

At every place setting there was a card listing the evening's menu:

> *Vegetable Soup à la Lake-wood*
> *Green Salad*
> *"Devine" Meatloaf*
> *Home-Style Mashed Potatoes*
> *Pecan Pie with Vanilla Ice Cream*
> *Coffee and Tea in the Living Room*

The Martins and McHughs sipped their soup. "Gosh, whom should we compliment?" said Mrs. McHugh.

"It says 'à la Lake-wood,' " Kate pointed out, her eyes twinkling. "That's Stevie *Lake* and Lisa *Atwood.*"

"Where are they?" Mr. Martin asked. "This is darned good soup."

"And he doesn't even like vegetables," his wife added.

Carole giggled. "I believe the chefs are in the kitchen."

At that moment the two girls emerged, carrying a large tureen. They were wearing white hats for the occasion.

"Anybody want seconds?" Stevie asked. She had insisted that there be enough for seconds of every course. After all, you had to treat others as you wanted to be treated yourself!

Lisa nudged her gleefully. Stevie looked up. Every hand at the table had gone up.

The meatloaf—made according to Phyllis Devine's secret recipe—was equally popular. Near the end of the main course, Lisa came out with her camera and took pictures of everyone enjoying the meal: the Martins, the McHughs, the Devines, the Brightstars, Carole, and Christine Lonetree. Earlier she had copied down the recipes for her home ec report. Everything was going like clockwork.

Just then Frank stood up to make a toast. "To our two cooks!" he said.

"Hear, hear!" called the table.

"And to their teacher!"

"Yay, Phyllis!"

"Yay, Mom!"

"And now," Frank continued more seriously, "I have another toast. As you all know, a few days ago, I bought five new horses. One of them didn't seem to like it here much. I predicted she'd settle in soon enough." He paused. He had the air of a man who has just made a major realization. When he continued, his voice was reflective. "But to tell you the truth, I'm not so sure she would have—if it hadn't been for a certain visitor. We have Carole Hanson to thank for giving us the black mare. By *giving* I mean acting as the liaison between the mare and us—me, the ranch—so that when Carole leaves, we can continue her training ourselves. Along the way . . ."

Kate's father had to stop again. Everyone at the table had burst into thunderous applause. Carole looked down at her plate. This was the last thing she had expected. A lecture, maybe, but a speech in her honor? Hardly!

"Ahem! Along the way," Frank continued, his face a mixture of respect and curiosity, "we noticed something peculiar. The mare had no name. It seems appropriate in a way, since she hadn't accepted humans. But now I'd like to announce that from here on"—he paused dramatically—"from here on, if Carole approves, the black mare will be known as Carole's Chance. Because if Carole hadn't taken a chance on her, nobody else would have. We would have treated her like any other horse. And as she proved two days ago, this mare is not any other horse."

Once again there was a burst of clapping and chatter. Only Carole was speechless. She didn't realize Frank had accepted that the mare was really and truly different. That was more important to her than any words of gratitude. He reached under the table and came up with a present. He handed it to her. Her hands shaking, Carole unwrapped it. She drew a brass rectangle out of the box. It was a nameplate to go on the door of the mare's stall. The inscription read CAROLE'S CHANCE. Carole's eyes were shining. Everyone was looking at her. She could never, ever put into words how she was feeling. She was incredibly thankful when Phyllis stood up. "Anyone ready for dessert?"

Stevie smiled with anticipation. "Sure, I'll have—" But she didn't get to finish her sentence. Beside her Lisa had clapped a hand to her forehead. Her mouth was open. Her eyes were nearly popping out of her head. Stevie felt her mouth go dry. Her limbs began to tremble.

The two girls pushed their chairs back from the table. They sprinted for the kitchen. Lisa flung open the oven door, expecting the worst.

"Why, oh, why! Why did we have to forget—" Lisa caught her breath.

Stevie looked to the heavens. "It's a miracle!" she cried.

The pies were absolutely perfect: golden brown crusts surrounding the dark pecan filling.

"I just don't get it," said Lisa, stunned with relief.

"You don't have to," Stevie replied, grabbing pot holders to remove the pies. "Our beautiful dessert has been saved. That's all that matters."

"But they were baking an extra twenty minutes at least," Lisa insisted. Then she noticed the dial on the oven. It was turned all the way down to a warming temperature. Lisa grinned. Suddenly she had an idea who had brought about the miracle.

"Girls, your guests are waiting," said a voice behind her. Phyllis had slipped into the kitchen after them.

"I know, I know, I'm bringing the pies out now," Stevie answered. "Lisa, grab the ice cream." She hurried out of the room.

"Say, Phyllis?" Lisa said.

"Yes?"

"Thanks."

Phyllis beamed. "Anytime," she said. She handed Lisa an ice cream scoop.

Lisa got the tub of vanilla out of the freezer. "Phyllis?" she said again, this time more thoughtfully.

"Yes?"

"How many times do you have to burn the dessert—or almost burn the dessert—to become a real cook?"

Smiling, Phyllis put an arm around Lisa's shoulder. "How many times do you have to fall off a horse to become a real rider?" she said.

Lisa laughed at the comparison. The first few times she'd fallen off, she had thought it was because she was a beginner. Then as she got better and still fell off occasionally, she'd thought it was because she was challenging herself more, with bigger jumps and more difficult horses. Now she realized that even the best riders fell sometimes. "A lot, huh?" she said to Phyllis.

Phyllis nodded. "And you haven't even begun to experiment with all the *other* disasters," she teased. "I mean, you've never dropped the pudding, or left out the baking soda, or had the dog get the steaks . . ."

Lisa's head began to spin. Phyllis turned her around. "Go," she said. "Go forth and conquer."

Stevie had served everyone pie in the living room. "Who's for ice cream?" Lisa asked.

Everyone but Carole put a hand up. Lisa noticed her friend standing at the edge of the group, looking wistfully at the door. When she was finished scooping ice cream, Lisa went over to her.

"Do you want to go see the mare—I mean," Lisa amended, "do you want to go see Carole's Chance?"

"I think we can call her Chance for short," Carole reassured her, laughing. "I'd feel strange if everyone was referring to her like that in front of me."

"Good," said Lisa, "because I would, too. Even though I love the name."

Stevie came over and joined them.

"And yeah," Carole answered, "I was thinking of going out and showing her her new nameplate."

"Great. We'll save you a piece of pie," Lisa said readily.

"Yes, tell her we say hello," said Stevie.

Carole frowned. "I was thinking maybe you guys would come with me," she said. "But if you don't want to—"

"Oh, no!" Stevie cried. "I mean, yes!"

"We'd love to!" exclaimed Lisa.

Carole looked at them. "I'm sorry, I—"

"We wish we had—"

"Next time we'll—"

All three of them stopped. Stevie opened her arms and they hugged one another. Some things didn't need explaining. What had happened, had happened. The important thing was that Carole was all right, and that Chance was all right. Laughing and gabbing, they headed for the door.

In the barn they met the most reassuring sign they could have seen: Chance was lying down in her stall. Stevie and Lisa looked at Carole. She beamed. Lying down was a big deal for a horse. It meant that she trusted her new environment enough to put herself in a helpless position, to let her guard down against attackers from the outside world. Wild horses hardly ever lay down.

Quietly the girls slipped into the stall. They patted Chance and scratched her withers. The mare was still a little nervous with people, but each encounter seemed to reassure her. Carole noted that she was friendlier with Lisa and Stevie than she had been with John, Mick, and Kate's father.

"You know, maybe I overreacted," Carole said reflectively, her arm around the mare's neck. "Maybe I shouldn't have gotten involved. But something made me do it. It was weird. It was as if I wasn't thinking. I was just doing—doing what I had to do." Even after the fact, she still didn't understand exactly what had made her try to set the mare free.

Stevie and Lisa glanced at one another in the semidarkness. Both of them were thinking about what John had said—that Carole had a special understanding of horses, that she was a horse whisperer. Somehow neither of them wanted to mention it. Somehow it seemed almost sacred, like something that should go unsaid.

"It's okay," Lisa said gently. "I'll bet you just knew how she was feeling more than anyone else did."

"Yeah. You were more in tune with her than other people," Stevie added.

Carole nodded, turning ideas over in her head. She thought back to the afternoon she had spent with the herd. Those horses had let her into their world. It was an experience she would never, ever forget. In a way it seemed more like a dream than reality.

It was strange, but sometimes Carole felt as if she had a special talent—or power or ability—for understanding horses. And not just for understanding them but for being able to communicate with them. She thought of saying something about it to Stevie and Lisa. It would be hard to explain, but she could try. But when she looked up and caught their eyes, she changed her mind. The way they were looking at her, it was almost as if they already knew.

ABOUT THE AUTHOR

Bonnie Bryant is the author of nearly a hundred books about horses, including The Saddle Club series, Saddle Club Super Editions, and the Pony Tails series. She has also written novels and movie novelizations under her married name, B. B. Hiller.

Ms. Bryant began writing The Saddle Club in 1986. Although she had done some riding before that, she intensified her studies then and found herself learning right along with her characters Stevie, Carole, and Lisa. She claims that they are all much better riders than she is.

Ms. Bryant was born and raised in New York City. She still lives there, in Greenwich Village, with her two sons.

Don't miss Bonnie Bryant's next exciting
Saddle Club adventure . . .

PAINTED HORSE
The Saddle Club #75

Stevie Lake is going on a class trip to New York City.
She can see herself hanging out in Greenwich Village,
but her teacher thinks long, boring lectures and a report are a much better idea. Well, Stevie has her own
plans. She shakes her classmates and sets off to explore
the Big Apple on her own. She ends up at the carousel
in Central Park, which she loves. She meets lots of
great people and horses—including a mounted police
officer.

When Stevie's class wanders into the park, they
don't have such a great adventure. In fact, they get
lost. Now it's up to Stevie and her new friends to save
them and stop the school trip from turning into a
disaster.